PRAISE FOR DA

'Do I recommend this book? Oh my dear sweet Jesus- I do! Nothing draws me into a book more than one that throws everything I love: crime, murders, serial killers, reality – into a story so well-written you have to wonder whether or not it happened. That is this book!'

CRIMEBOOKJUNKIE.CO.UK

'Nameless occupies the realms of horror / thriller and doesn't hold back.'

LITTLE BOOKNESS LANE

'David McCaffrey is a fantastic writer… he tells us exactly what we need to know about the previous outings of these characters without spoiling the pace of this one. Not an easy skill but one which McCaffrey pulls off effortlessly. I was totally absorbed by Nameless - the characters, the plot, the twists, the turns, the pace, the descriptives… all leading to many WOW moments!'

EMMA THE LITTLE BOOK WORM

'If you're looking for a crime thriller with a difference and a book that really makes you think about topics that matter, I can't recommend this book highly enough.'

- MARK TILBURY, AUTHOR OF THE ABATTOIR OF DREAMS AND THE LIAR'S PROMISE

NAMELESS

DAVID MCCAFFREY

First published in 2017 by:
Britain's Next Bestseller
An imprint of Live It Ventures LTD
27 Old Gloucester Road
London.
WC1N 3AX
www.bnbsbooks.co.uk
This edition Copyright © 2018 by David McCaffrey

@BNBSbooks
www.davidmccaffrey.net
ISBN 978-1-910565-84-1
Cover designed by Rowland Kell

DEDICATIONS

To those who taught me the true meaning of the word
betrayal –
Thank you

To those who taught me the true meaning of the word
loyalty –
Thank you

ACKNOWLEDGMENTS

As is customary these days, I can't proceed without thanking my friend, mentor and bestselling author, Steve Alten. I would not have *Nameless* nor any other books under my belt if not for him.

Murielle Maupoint – she gave me my shot, supported me in so many ways and believed in my wife and I so much that she sold us her company! Kelly and I will always do all we can to make her proud.

Siobhan, my proof reader – thank you for keeping me right.

Bob Tibbitts – typesetter extraordinaire, deserves a special mention.

A huge thank you to so many amazing people – Muffin, Sarah, Emma Mitchell, Gordon, Rebecca Sill, Steve Wraith, Stephen Sayers, Paul, Andy and Kev, all the girls at Crime Book Club for their support and encouragement, everyone at The Book Club (especially the force of nature that is Tracy Fenton), Lou Lou, Donna, Maxamillions,

Julie T, Lisa Eddom, Jacky Collins, Vic Watson... I've probably forgotten loads of names so I apologise, but you're fantastic wherever you are!

Silviya Yordanova who designed the amazing cover for Nameless - you are awesome. Her website Dark Imaginarium is one to check out for first-class covers.

Special thanks goes to Simone for her web design, pestering and all around talent! Thank you!

My beautiful Turtle and amazing children, Jakey and Gruffy, whom I wouldn't be here without.

My Mum because she's my Mum and my brothers, John, Alan and Patrick.

A very special thank you to Dianne Bowden who has helped me in ways I could never fully show appreciation for.

The same goes to Claire Davies, Neil Holmes, Angie Boyes, Jo Dunmore, Paula Atkin, Jill Wingham, Tom Jacques, Deborah Shotton, Richard Bellamy, Lisa Reamsbottom, Sharon Lance, Gill Postgate, Alison Peevor, Amy Dent and especially Helen Brown. You stood by me without question and your belief never wavered.

And finally you, the readers. Your support and encouragement is without measure.

Thank you and know this author only exists because of you.

'*Deep into that darkness peering, long I stood there, wondering, fearing, doubting, dreaming dreams no mortal ever dared to dream before.*'

Edgar Allen Poe

'*There is no hunting like the hunting of man, and those who have hunted armed men long enough and liked it, never care for anything else thereafter.*'

Ernest Hemingway

PROLOGUE

NOW

"GO FUCK YOURSELF."

Those had been Joe O'Connell's last words before finding himself here.

Drifting back from unconsciousness, he returned from darkness only to find himself engulfed in a different kind— one that was virtually pitch black and imbued with a musty, dank smell.

He tried to lift himself from the seated position he was in, straining against the leather straps securing him in place. Iron ankle fetters tethered his legs tightly against what he recognised was a chair. His fingers felt around the arms to see if he could create any give in the straps but he gave up after a minute or so. Something cold and hard was pressing against the soles of his feet. It took him a few moments to realise his shoes and socks had been removed and that the stone floor was the source of the chill.

Adrenaline shot through his body, jolting him back into a hyper-aware state. His muscles, though appearing to be unresponsive, had retained their innate ability to twitch and contract, causing him to shiver in the chill of the air.

His memory sluggish, he briefly recalled where he had been before here—the house— and remembered the pressure of the needle as it had punctured the skin of his neck and the soft call of insentience as it engulfed him.

Joe began to writhe about violently with no effect. The chair remained static as though fastened to the floor. His eyes were still adjusting to the gloom of his surroundings. He screwed them up a few times to see if it would help him focus and make sense of anything.

He was able to discern his location was either a storage container or perhaps a huge silo. There were slatted windows on either side but no light through them, meaning either they were covered or it was night-time.

It felt like night, though he couldn't articulate why. Perhaps his somnolent state was due to the residual effects of whatever he'd been sedated with to get him here. As if on cue, the injection site began to throb and he attempted to angle his neck in order to rub it against his shoulder. It wasn't as effective as scratching with a finger, but it would have to do. Joe knew he had much bigger problems to worry about.

Part of him wondered whether he was dreaming. That he was somehow in the middle of a nightmare he was yet to wake from. Recent events rolled around his mind - Etchison, the Branch Obadians - as he considered the life choices that had led to this.

Being here. In this room.

As a child, he had always been terrified of the dark. Nyctophobia.

The word itself had always reminded him of a creature lurking within the night's obsidian embrace. A nyctophobe… a nyctosaur. He had come up with all sorts of names for them. Supine creatures that lurked beneath your bed or in the wardrobe.

It was rising now, the grinding anxiety that accompanied that fear, the most basic of limiting mechanisms to prevent reckless behaviour in the most extreme of circumstances. An evolutionary advantage which prevented you from running around the African desert like a lunatic when there were lions present.

His fear of the dark had never prompted an acute fight or flight response. Instead, it had always developed more like a foreboding prescience, creeping up from the base of his spine and slowly enveloping his chest like an anaconda squeezing the very breath from his body. Ironically, that increasing anxiety also augmented situational awareness, making someone finely attuned to environmental cues when their wellbeing might be in danger.

No shit.

Fear—a gnawing emotion, honed over millennia by both nature and nurture so that it became a systemic and instinctive survival response that could prepare you for the world and ensure that you would intuitively do whatever you needed to do to survive - to live another day.

Or die another day.

Either way, fear was the body's way of making certain you never forgot what was needed to go on living. Oddly, none of that was helpful as Joe sat here with a hunch that what was about to follow would be painful and possibly fatal. An old Simon and Garfunkel lyric inexplicably popped into his head relating to the welcoming of darkness.

He heard breathing in the obscurity before a light blinked on above him, causing phosphenes to appear in bursts before his eyes. His vision blurred, and he could just make out someone standing in front of a table at the end of the room. He could also make out the figure patiently laying out a variety of medical implements that Joe knew weren't there to help him with his ingrowing toenail.

The stranger who had brought him here was built like a rugby player, the muscles on his arms threatening to rip through his tightly buttoned black jacket.

"So, that's how far we've come," announced the man gently in a soft British accent, his back to Joe. "Heroism has gone from a rallying cry or profound statement to *'go fuck yourself?'* And you call yourself a journalist. Shame on you."

"Get bent," Joe snorted derisively, straining futilely once again at his restraints.

"You've the potential to cause me a great deal of trouble, Joseph. I wanted to kill you back at the house. Maybe I did and you're in Hell."

His right hand floated over the various items as though trying to decide which one to choose. Settling on a scalpel, he turned back to face Joe, his face hidden in the shadows.

"You know, I met Obadiah Stark," Joe stated emphatically. "I can already tell you're a rank amateur compared to him. I don't even think you'd be interesting enough to make him sick."

The man stepped forward and pressed the scalpel against the right-hand side of Joe's neck in a swift motion. His black hair was cut close to his head, flashes of grey along the temple. Freckles peppered his tanned face, vivid blue eyes belaying clarity of purpose. His mouth was turned up slightly as though trying to force a smile.

"This area I'm pressing against is called Erb's point, named after Wilhelm Heinrich Erb who located it. It's basically where the four nerves of the cervical plexus meet. And if I just make a small incision here…"

Joe cried out as the scalpel slid into his neck, severing the nerve cluster with the immediate effect of making his right arm tingle as though immersed in freezing cold water. He felt it go limp, his hand automatically rotating and flexing up over as though gesturing for a tip.

"…you'll find you're paralysed down your right arm. Incidentally, this injury affects the circulation, which means your arm will no longer be able to regulate its temperature, so in cold weather, it'll hurt like a son of a bitch."

Joe grimaced against the pain migrating from his neck and up and down his right side. His body shook with adrenaline, though he imagined his old friend fear was also playing a part.

"It's funny," the stranger said, his voice lilting softly. "I've never actually killed anyone before. Never even laid a finger on those cattle I procure for my clients. You would be my first… breaking me in so to speak. Your knowledge has the potential to damage my reputation. It's that reputation which has contributed to the confidence of my clientele in dealing with me, knowing I'll provide them with a superior product, exactly as requested. And I have no intention of letting you FUCK IT ALL UP!"

The man began shaking, hitting himself on the head in frustration. Joe couldn't help but smile at the fact that his apparent existence, despite the pain and fear he felt, were having such a profound effect. He just wished he knew who his assailant was.

"So what happens now?" Joe asked glibly. "I say sorry, tell you I won't say anything, you let me go with my limp arm and we call it quits?"

"I admire your ability to find humour, even in such a despairing state," the stranger announced, the angry tremble in his voice rapidly receding. "It's endearing actually. But you know what's about to happen. You'll be tortured and tell me something I want to know."

"Which is what exactly?" Joe countered.

"The truth. And I have something that'll help you locate it."

He stepped back to the table and swapped the scalpel for a series of bamboo slivers before moving to the back of the room out of Joe's sight.

The sound of a chair being dragged echoed around the room before the man reappeared and sat down, rocking the chair forward slightly so that they were directly in front of each other. He ran a finger along the tops of the bamboo, the motion making a barely audible clicking sound that Joe found extremely disturbing.

Joe felt sweat building up on the back of his neck, his increasing respirations causing him to feel lightheaded. Joe realised his irrational fear of the dark had been just a minor apprehension compared to this. If he didn't know better, he would have said he was having a panic attack. Joe suddenly found himself wondering if it was possible to die from fear.

The man selected one of the bamboo slivers, placing the others on the table to his left. He positioned it just below the index finger nail of Joe's right hand.

"In case you haven't guessed yet, this is going to hurt… a lot."

'Obsession is the single most wasteful human activity, because with an obsession you keep coming back and back and back to the same question and never get an answer.'

Norman Mailer

FEBRUARY 18TH 21:57

Two weeks earlier

The rain pounded unrelentingly over Tralee Bay, causing the boats berthed in the marina to undulate gently one after the other.

Joe sat crossed-legged by the window, oblivious to the severe weather besieging his house and the adjacent residences. Surrounding him were scattered papers, newspaper articles, photographs and reports. To the casual observer, it would have appeared that their placement was random, but they were meticulously arranged into a specific order.

He took a big mouthful of Jack Daniels – neat, only ice to taint it – and placed the glass beside him. It was the first drink he'd had in months. Not that he'd ever been an alcoholic, but he'd discovered some time ago that if he continued with the excuse he was only a social drinker, he would slip down a slope he hadn't realised he was skiing on. Smoking, on the other hand, was something he did too much of and had no intention of giving up. It always helped calm him.

Joe lit up a cigarette and drew on it deeply, scratching at four days of stubble on his face. After a few more drags, he placed it in the ashtray and rested back onto his elbows, letting out a huge sigh of frustration. What he needed was here somewhere. He just needed to look with better eyes.

Some investigative journalist, he chided.

It all seemed so long ago that Joe often found himself wondering if it had been real. After all, it was so vast and conspiratorial that it sounded like the plot of a crime thriller.

But it was real. There was an organisation hiding beneath the veneer of altruism and beneficence while pulling the strings of many government officials, politicians, police officers, lawyers and members of the justice system.

They had conspired, cajoled, betrayed and even murdered, all under the banner of reorganising the social strata so that the world could find itself again.

Machiavelli would have been proud.

For four years now, Joe had been investigating The Brethren, always mindful of their threat to his life but unable to let go. How could he? He had been at the centre of what would be, if made public, the largest conspiracy ever reported. Serial killers falsely executed so they could be privately tortured in order to satisfy the desires of those who felt the justice system had failed them. And he suspected that was only the tip of their obfuscatory iceberg. The magnitude of it was beyond comprehension, and yet Joe knew that life's sense of irony would find many people probably in support of their actions.

Obadiah Stark had been a monster, of that there was no doubt. Even facing his death for the second time, he had been unrepentant for the 27 murders he'd committed.

Yet Joe had seen something else in him, not humanity, but perhaps realisation. Maybe even an acceptance of how his individualised suffering had shown him something unique. He had to admit the technology The Brethren had employed to carry out their own brand of restorative justice was impressive. Drugs and a *deus ex machina* designed to tailor one's suffering to meet a specific request.

The threat to him had been clear—investigate and he would find himself *in extremis*, suffering in ways most likely unimaginable. So he had done it anyway, but furtively. And after leaving *The Daily Eire*, Joe had found he'd had an abundance of time on his hands to devote to the project.

His first thread had been to try and locate Vicky, but that had drawn a blank. E-mails and bank accounts deleted, phone numbers disconnected. Only a Google search of her name pointed towards evidence she ever existed at all. Even her sister, Sara, was nowhere to be found.

Using his connections in the FBI, Kev O'Hagan had helped him uncover bits and pieces, the most interesting of which insinuated that The Brethren had been somehow involved with the Whitechapel murders more than one hundred years ago. Hospital records he had obtained purported that one Thomas Quinn, a resident of a workhouse in London and former employee of The Brethren, had known the identity of Jack the Ripper and that he had worked for them.

Joe had initially found the whole idea ridiculous, but the fact that The Brethren were mentioned in a century old document had made him consider that it was too much of a historical coincidence.

Other documents from the period reported them as saviours of the downtrodden and legally mistreated, the familiarity of which resonated with Joe like the acutest sense of *déja vu*. They'd been up to their tricks, even back then. Perhaps that was where it had all begun.

Joe tried hard to contain the sudden rage he felt, recalling their manipulation of him - Vicky's betrayal - as he rose to his feet and took his glass into the kitchen for a top up. He grabbed the bottle and was about to pour when he hesitated. This is exactly what he didn't want to be doing, losing control and objectivity when that was all he had left. He screwed the cap back on the Jack Daniels and gave it a defiant tap before placing it back in the cupboard. He had just dropped the glass in the sink when the phone rang.

Joe collected the cordless extension from where he stood in the kitchen.

"Hello."

"Joe," Andrew Phillips stated on the other end. "I think I have something you'll be really, really interested in."

"Well don't keep me in suspense, Andy," Joe replied.

"We've just found a woman's body in Ballyseedy Woods."

"Wow, that is fascinating," Joe said with less feeling than he'd intended. Andy was one of his friends in the Gardaí, going back before the Stark murders. He had always been a good source of information, treading that fine line between his duty as an officer and being a friend.

"No, that's not the interesting part," Andy replied, ignoring Joe's glib reply. "We arrested someone at the scene, an as yet unidentified woman."

"And?" Joe idly glanced at the ashtray, mentally noting he would need to light another cigarette.

"… and she has a tattoo on her back. A tattoo consisting of tally marks."

"Tally marks…" Joe repeated quietly, a sense of foreboding wrapping itself around his entire body.

"But that's not the only thing," Andy continued. "She said she'd only speak to you."

'Whoever has not stood in the grave-yard on the summit of that cliff among the beehive dwellings and beehive oratory does not know Ireland through and through.'

George Bernard Shaw

||

Lamont Etchison believed in intensity. Strength, power and concentration - attributes one needed for pure intensity.

He had learnt it from an early age. Born into a working class and unremarkable family, his parents had held basic jobs. His mother, Bonnie, had been a teacher at Blackrock College in Dublin; his father a worker at Inchicore Locomotive Works.

Qualified in the most minimal way, they had led a simple life and brought Lamont up the same. They taught him that life was there to be embraced and enjoyed. His childhood was basically happy, it was sad, but that was it. Moments of drama were absent, as was change. Life occurred, one moment after another without breaks or moments of interruption.

He recalled the occasion he'd received a phone call from the hospital, telling him his mother had just passed away from the cancer that had been slowly eating away at her body for months. Lamont had jumped in his car, heading for the hospital and had then turned off onto another road before he'd arrived and just kept going - never seeing his father again nor his mother's body. To him, it was just a mundane, daily event and not a life-changing moment. His sense of history at that moment was symbolic. It made him realise that the inscription of our life is a series of discontinuities. He had no sense of history.

For Lamont Etchison, it didn't exist.

He lay on his bed, listening to the sound of the wind whistling across the dusk-imbued landscape. He could hear the sound of laughter upstairs from one of the gatherings taking place tonight. He had considered joining them but decided against it. They needed these opportunities to find some release from the intensity of their duties.

There it was again. Intensity.

Lamont didn't believe in an afterlife. He believed in the here and now. The work he had been tasked with was to ensure that when his time was up, the world would understand what it was he was trying to do. What it was *he* had tried to do. They didn't understand how Stark's personality was one that nature had deemed important enough to ensure that it could be used to serve mankind in its struggle to survive.

His high-end philosophies on life and death had driven Lamont towards recognising his own apotheosis, knowing that this mission would ensure he rose above mere mortals and facilitate his transformation into something like *him*— without pity, remorse or limits.

Stark had known that the world and those living in it were subject to the march of reality. It was what governed their belief systems and ultimately what made them weak. Lamont had been instructed to encourage the Branch Obadians that there was no time; that they were all living in the now. He believed that if they just let themselves go, they could access a power that could change the course of history. Stark had said it himself—sharks, lions and tigers all have senses designed to seek out the wheat from the chaff. Lamont had been told it still needed to be done.

What The Branch would help them achieve.

He didn't see himself as a killer. He preferred to see himself as an auteur, recreating life on a canvas as he saw fit - human bodies being the easels, the canvas being flesh, the implements the Obadians. As for the rest, it was simple. Do as you're told, follow the plan and you'll be rewarded. That was what he'd been promised. Cocaine, reading, women and devotion kept him stable and focused. He knew that he was only ever a step away from disparate rage and the compelling desires that would see him caught and arrested. This way, using the Branch, he could indulge himself when he saw fit and live his dream through them.

He had been given an amazing gift, an opportunity few could appreciate. Why he had been chosen he didn't know but believed it would be unwise to question it too much.

Stark had known that living the way he had allowed him to get more out of himself and that by seeing his inner soul from a different perspective, one of a messiah bringing peace to the lost and those tired of living, he could be alternate from the rest. Lamont saw, as Stark had believed, that people needed to die so that others could be reborn in their stead.

Perhaps the world would see the Branch - the Obadians -

as a religion, possibly a society. Some might even use the word *cult*. But Lamont knew it was more. He saw them as Gnostic, a religion that had chosen to follow a doctrine of salvation based upon Obadiah Stark's teachings so that they might drive the world towards a process of awakening. He believed that human nature and impulses were a reflection of our basic desires and beliefs.

Lamont's master knew as Stark had, that society was broken and that human beings lacked the understanding of the power they could hold. His mission was to demonstrate that power. And through The Branch, he could. They would prove that the God the world believed it was simply a demiurge, a lesser and inferior false god. He would show them that Stark had seen the truth of this world and what it took to bring it into a new age—one of understanding and realisation.

Lamont understood that these things were only possible through sacrifice and suffering. One had to walk through the fire in order to come out purified on the other side. And he had people around him who would help achieve this.

Knowledge of Obadiah Stark hadn't been a prerequisite to joining, but an appreciation of his philosophy had to be apparent once indoctrinated. Followers had to be willing to do whatever was asked of them without question. Correction upwards was tantamount to rebellion and would not be tolerated.

Susan Bradley had been one of their most devoted. She had been with them since the beginning and, Lamont had thought, demonstrated a true understanding of Stark's truth. Her resistance to doing what needed to be done had been a surprise, especially when he knew she'd been open to his demands before. Her threats to go to the authorities had come as even more of a shock.

Maybe he had misjudged her. Perhaps she'd never really left her old life behind. Her death, however, had provided an opportunity. Granted, he hadn't expected to execute that phase so soon, but it mattered little. Once the message was received, their plan would truly begin.

Deciding he would join the group after all, Lamont rose from his bed and moved towards the stairs. He caught sight of himself in the mirror and paused to study his reflection.

At fifty-eight years old, he thought he looked well. Only his grey hair, cropped closely to his scalp, threatened to betray his age. His green eyes projected a ferocity matched only by his keen intellect. He pulled down on his white shirt and brushed the front of his black trousers.

Image was everything. It complimented his ideals of discipline and precision. Without mastery, chaos would soon follow. For this vision to be successful, all who followed had to be obedient. Stark had remained successful for so long only because he respected patience and manipulation. Lamont admired such qualities.

He smiled at the ambiguity he knew their actions would bring. The person behind the curtain, manipulating it all, remained nameless. Lamont felt sorry for humanity, knowing what was to come. He felt sorry for the one he had been told about. The one who held the key.

The one who would learn all too late that everything comes at a cost.

'Do you think the universe fights for souls to be together? Some things are too strange and strong to be coincidences.'

Emery Allen

JOE TOOK A LARGE SWIG OF COFFEE WHILST HE GLANCED around, watching the uniformed bodies of Kenmare Gardaí Station weave their way between desks and each other.

High visibility jackets, ballistic anti-stab vests surrounded him, the buzzing of a dozen voices all seemingly talking at once to whoever was on the other end of their mobile phone filling the room. The atmosphere was so thick with emotion and activity it was almost manifesting itself as a physical presence. He had never seen the effect a zero priority job could have on individuals devoted to protecting the public. And there was something else in the air that took him a moment to recognise, mixed in with the smell of body odour and coffee.

Desperation.

His thoughts drifted towards old friends at the paper and he felt momentary loss at the void losing his job there had left in his life. Alison, Ciaran… even David, despite the fact he was a complete tosser. They had all been part of his daily routine for so long that he had struggled to rebalance himself after everything that happened.

He didn't think reporters could suffer from PTSD but apparently, so his therapist had informed him, it wasn't uncommon for anyone having witnessed or experienced a traumatic event in which physical harm occurred or was threatened to suffer certain emotions. He guessed that having had flashbacks to being sat opposite the world's worst serial killer whilst being threatened with death by a powerful and omnipresent conglomerate probably covered that. He had certainly relived a few moments following the phone call last night, checking all the windows and door locks an extra two times on top of the usual four before bed.

Remembering his sudden burst of fear and helplessness last night only hastened the fatigue that had been enveloping his body. Ultimately, he hadn't been able to sleep and had instead spent his time poring over the details of the murder and, more interestingly, the accused.

The as yet unidentified suspect had been found sat beside the body of the as yet unidentified victim. The weather last night had been bitter and windy, yet Andy said she had appeared unaffected by the cold. A knife clenched in her hand, she had not resisted arrest nor said a word. They had taken her into custody and placed her in a dry cell. Even though the circumstantial evidence was damning, it was procedure to place the suspect in a 'dry cell' where they had no access to water and therefore wouldn't be able to remove any DNA evidence before officers got the chance to take samples.

Swabs, photographs and fingerprints had been taken, the

latter of which they were hoping would provide them with her identity. She had remained silent the entire time, not even saying anything when the Force's Medical Examiner had performed his psychological and physiological assessment to establish her health and state of mind. Yet despite all of this the part that fascinated Joe the most was her body, specifically the tattoo on her back.

His being here was purely at the sufferance of the Chief Inspector and the investigative officers. He had been reluctantly provided with the file in front of him because it was recognised that his knowledge of Obadiah Stark and former employment as a journalist, alongside his being specifically asked for, might generate an observation they could potentially overlook.

Joe could sense the animosity at his being in amongst the men and women who would be working day and night investigating the murder whilst he sat at home, safe and sound under the blanket of the security they provided. In order to counteract the emotions around him, Joe intended to make himself as useful as possible.

He flipped to the front of the folder and slowly turned a photograph around, as though slow manipulation would reveal something previously unseen. Taken when she'd been examined, the tattoo was an exact approximation of Obadiah Stark's, right down to the tally marks where there should be an epitaphic. Hers numbered only four, whereas Stark's had represented 27 dead souls.

In this case, what do they represent?

Turning his attention to the victim, he spread the numerous photographs of the deceased woman's body out in front of him. Scanning over the coroner's report, Joe noted she had been found with a fractured arm, multiple stab wounds to her body, stab wounds inside her mouth, mutilation of her ears, nose, mouth, lips and genitalia, both eyes had been gouged out with stab wounds to the empty eye sockets and it appeared she'd been partially scalped.

Even to a layman like Joe, he could see this wasn't just a random killing. It had been personal. The victim had been deliberately mutilated, probably to teach her a lesson and more than likely to send a message to a specific individual or individuals.

Joe placed the victim's photograph back on top of the others and pursed his lips. His journalistic instinct told him that the fact a woman who had an exact replica of The Tally Man's tattoo on her back had murdered someone was not a coincidence. It meant something specific. He just didn't know what… yet.

It was only as he went to flick the folder closed that he saw it on her back. It was barely noticeable on the photograph, initially appearing to be part of the tattoo. Peering closer he saw that it appeared to be a small, raised area about the size of a watch face right between her shoulder blades.

He felt a chill ripple over him.

If he didn't know better, Joe would have said something had been stitched beneath her skin.

'Sometimes human places, create inhuman monsters'

Stephen King

THE SUN SHONE AS LAMONT MADE HIS WAY TOWARDS THE makeshift altar.

The congregation, a mixture of men and women, awaited him. Some shuffled from side to side impatiently, others quietly conversed with their neighbour. But all became attentive the moment he stood before them. He had instructed them to come to the island because he believed that standing here, where history itself held sway, they would truly know what it meant to preside over everything.

Craggy and vertiginous, Skellig Michael's sense of isolation and forbidding location only helped strengthen what he was trying to do here. 714 feet above sea level with only six beehive huts, two oratories and small terraces to represent the potential for civilisation, the island had accommodated

Vikings and monks amongst its illustrious guests. All had believed that enduring the island allowed for an enlightenment that was only accessible through the hardship and suffering it offered. Its importance during Pagan times was legendary. Alongside a history of kings seeking to rule and saints fleeing persecution, the very island resonated with history and potency.

He nodded to those gathered before him, taking in every face standing in his thrall. Lamont knew they were devoted. Some had given him their body. All had given him their souls. They stood to attention, waiting for him to speak. It was in these moments that he felt the power and understood how Obadiah must have felt, like a leviathan in a world of the unenlightened. Nothing could compare to the discernment that every human being before you was willing to live and die at your command.

"I stand here with nothing to prove. You have seen what we can accomplish. We have lost two of our own… Susan had to be sacrificed in order to secure our future, Rebecca had to be the one to deliver the message; a burden she shouldered with honour and dignity. Susan came to us a believer but lost her way… fell from the path and became a reflection of who she used to be. Through her sacrifice, she became a beacon to show others our true power."

A few of the congregation murmured in agreement, others just nodded.

"A reckoning approaches my family. Obadiah knew it. I know it. We, the real strong, have no need to prove it to anyone, but we will show them anyway. Stark's teachings edified us, showing us that the human cattle think they are in charge. But they are not. We will show them that in order to balance the social strata, we will go forth and continue his message… only we will do it better. Where he failed, we will succeed.

"Stark knew the world wasn't meant to be this way. They have become lost in their own desires, solipsism and arrogance. His message, once powerful, has now been disregarded and lost. We will ensure it is heard again. No longer shall we delay gratification. We shall move forward and cleanse the land from the filth that has sullied it so. They will learn you cannot walk away from the lessons Stark was trying to teach. They must be endured and understood. I know you will not fail me. We must go forward and show the world what we are truly capable of. We need to show them that there is great power in Stark's original culling of 27 and that only with such an accomplishment will this insipid world see the message he began so long ago."

Cheers and acknowledgement of his words filled the air, the wind doing little to dampen their resonance.

"They will say we are evil. That what we are doing is unspeakable and horrific. But what is evil? It is such an intrinsic property that it cannot ever be truly defined. We are but the vicious mole of nature that Hamlet spoke of to Horatio. Good and evil, day and night… coexistent harmonies that form part of one another. And with harmony comes balance. That is what we are demonstrating to those who choose to listen. The world can have its guidelines and generalities for good and evil. But the meaning of a word is its usage. Our calling is not driven by evil, but illumination. We shall light the way and show the blasphemers that there is only one truth. Stark's truth… that of purity of the flesh."

As he finished speaking a few of the women moved towards him, their faces filled with desire and anticipation. Lamont rolled his head through a circle to work the kinks out of his neck as he considered taking them right here. He imagined it would be a unique experience, accentuated by the history and power of the location. Perks of his role. He didn't think his master would mind.

Yes, Lamont thought. *Obadiah Stark will live once again and all will fear his name.*

'If you prick us do we not bleed? If you tickle us do we not laugh? If you poison us do we not die? And if you wrong us shall we not revenge?'

William Shakespeare

EVEN JOE FELT EXPOSED AS HE VIEWED THE MONITORS showing the inside of the interrogation room, or 'The Box' as Andy had called it.

The unfamiliarity and sense of isolation were palpable, even from his side, though he knew that was the point. Ensure that the physical layout of the room was such that it would maximise the suspect's discomfort and sense of powerlessness from the moment they stepped inside. Provide them with an uncomfortable chair, ensure the walls of the room are blank and make certain they can't reach anything. Joe knew it was all to set up a feeling of dependence.

At this moment in time the suspect, who had been identified as Rebecca Sill, didn't look at all dependent. Her expression was one of serenity. Given the circumstances in which she had been found, Joe found that odd to say the least. And just the slightest bit sinister. Even the solicitor who had been assigned to her looked uncomfortable. She hadn't asked for one, it was just procedure to protect her rights. He'd overheard Rebecca being advised not to say anything unless instructed to, and had been slightly amused by the blasé look she had fired back in response to the instruction. If the ground could have opened up before her, Joe imagined the solicitor would have gladly jumped in headfirst.

He had been given permission to watch the interrogation only because his name had been specifically mentioned and Andy had vouched for him. Though the superintendent and a majority of the officers knew him from his journalism days, he was still only a civilian and civilians were kept on a very short leash when it came to being in a police station. He was keeping the detail he had seen in the photograph to himself for the time being. He had a funny feeling no one else had spotted it with all that was going on.

Two detective inspectors Joe recognised as Alexandria Barclay and Heather Robinson entered the room. Heather, the Senior Investigating Officer and coordinator took the seat facing the suspect. Alex, the Deputy SIO moved towards the one in the corner by the table where the DVD equipment for recording interviews was positioned and removed her jacket before sitting down. Sitting as they were, the suspect would have to keep turning to look at them. Again, all intended to increase a suspect's anxiety.

Rebecca glanced up at the location of the two cameras and smiled, as though she knew Joe was watching. A shiver slithered up his back at her almost seductive expression before she turned her attention back the officers.

Heather turned on the recorder. "The time is 09: 48, the date February 19th, Interview Room 5. Detective Inspector Heather Robinson present with colleague Detective

Inspector Alex Barclay. Also present is solicitor Sue Hargreaves."

Rebecca remained impassive, moving to rest her chin on the palm of her left hand. Heather continued.

"Rebecca, let me explain the process. I'm going to start off by getting some background information from you and then we will talk in a little more detail about what happened last night. Do you understand?"

Rebecca glanced up but her expression remained emotionless. Heather shot a brief look at Alex that seemed to indicate they knew they were in for a hard time.

"Are you responsible for killing that woman?"

"I'll only speak to Joe O'Connell," Rebecca responded.

"What knowledge do you have of that person and how they died?" Heather pressed, ignoring her statement.

Rebecca remained silent.

"Why were you at the scene of the crime?" Greeted by silence and a nonchalant look, Heather continued. "Where were you prior to being in Ballyseedy Woods?"

"I'll only speak to Joe O'Connell," Rebecca repeated whilst glancing at the floor as though looking for something.

"Joe O'Connell is a civilian. He isn't allowed to speak to the prime suspect in a murder case."

"Well, in that case I have nothing more to say to you, as I'll only speak to O'Connell. But because I feel a little sorry for you both and you're trying so hard I'll throw you a bone. Shoot?"

Her voice was firm, with no hint of anxiety. The Northern Irish accent only accentuated her resolve.

"Did you kill that woman?" Heather asked again.

"Susan Bradley?" Rebecca queried. "Yes. Did I mutilate her? Absolutely. Why? Because she had to be taught a lesson."

"And what was the lesson, Rebecca?" Heather asked, looking incredulously at Alex.

"The lesson of consequences. She refused to do what was asked of her… she was punished."

"And what was it she had been asked to do?"

Rebecca's mouth curled slightly at the edges. "She was supposed to kill someone for our cause. She refused, so she died. Really, really slowly. I would have filmed it but have you ever tried wielding a knife whilst trying to record yourself? No mean feat I tell you."

"And you did this under instruction?"

"Of course," Rebecca replied, affecting a mock-arrogant tone that reminded Joe of Bane's response to the FBI agent in The Dark Knight Rises.

"Who gave the order?" Heather asked.

Rebecca burst into laughter, exaggerating her amusement just long enough to make the detectives in the room feel uncomfortable. Even Joe felt himself cringe at her faux merriment.

"Well played, detective. Of course I'm going to tell you who told me to kill her. You've broken me down to such a point that I cannot see things clearly and feel the need to get specific details off my chest and that weight off my shoulders. Oh, you are both far too good. And far too inept to even comprehended the magnitude of it all."

"How do you know the victim?"

Rebecca's mouth curled up slightly at the edges, not so much a smile but more like a crocodile grin. She imitated the sound of a loud buzzer before speaking. "Sorry, your time's up. Thank you for playing. Now in case I wasn't clear the first three times, J.O.E O' C.O.N.N.E.L.L."

Heather ignored Rebecca's arrogant and deliberate pronunciation of the name, but still felt herself flushed with embarrassment at her patronising tone. Hardness had entered Rebecca's eyes, which Heather knew meant she would get little without offering something. She looked at the solicitor with a stare that said 'you should be doing something about this. It's in your client's best interests.' Sue Hargreaves looked away uncomfortably.

Nodding to Alex, both detectives rose from their seats and left the room. Neither acknowledged Rebecca nor her solicitor on their way out. A few moments later they entered the room where Joe currently stood.

Alex silently moved to the corner, never taking her eyes off Joe. He felt her mistrust of the whole situation coming off her in waves and crashing into him. He couldn't blame her. His name had been the first thing she'd said upon her arrest. Understandably they wanted to know why and how, if at all, he was involved. When it came down to it, so did he.

Heather marched up to Joe until they were so close his nose was almost touching hers. He could smell the perfume on her skin. Armani Diamonds if he wasn't mistaken.

"I need to take this higher. I can't just let you in there because she asks for it. And the only reason I'm entertaining this nonsense is because she just implied there's more to all of this. If she means more victims then we need to know what she knows. If you have to be the intermediary then fine, I'll play for now. Stay here."

Heather moved towards the door, turning to face Alex as she left.

"Make certain he doesn't leave," she instructed, pointing at Joe as she walked out.

Twenty minutes had passed before Heather returned with the solicitor in tow.

Rebecca had spent the entire time humming 'If You Go Down to the Woods Today' in a slow, creepy manner, occasionally glancing up at the cameras and smiling. It was as though she knew her request was going to be granted.

"You get five minutes. You don't touch her, you don't negotiate with her and be very careful with the questions you ask."

Heather jabbed a finger at the solicitor. "You'll be in there too." A hesitant nod was her only response.

"Alex'll be watching and listening from here," she continued. "Just because the captain thinks you're hot shit over the Stark thing, doesn't make it so. Do you understand me?"

"Absolutely," Joe acknowledged. "Look, I'm as curious as you are to know why she asked for me."

"Do you recognise her?" Heather asked. "Nope, never seen her before."

"And the tattoo. What do you make of that?"

Joe studied Rebecca on the monitor for a few moments before responding. "I'm not sure. Obadiah Stark's tattoo was unique in the sense that it stood for something personal to him. Why anyone would want to copy it is beyond me. It's not like he was capable of setting a trend like David Beckham."

Heather studied Joe, trying to work out if he was genuine. "Well, I have a hunch that her asking for you and having *that* on her back are related. Fuckin' Obadiah Stark. Even dead the guy causes nothing but trouble."

Joe couldn't help but smile. "Yeah, I recall thinking that myself a long time ago."

Heather motioned for Alex to escort Joe and Sue into the room. The detective opened the door, gesturing for them to move through first.

"Ladies first," Joe said.

Alex grunted a response but moved ahead of Joe and Sue. He followed them both around the corner and stood before the door leading into the interrogation room.

Once more unto the breech, he thought as he turned the handle and walked through the door.

Rebecca stared long and hard at Joe, her face lifeless as though working out the correct emotion to convey.

Mercury-red hair spilled down over her shoulders, its unkempt texture only helping to accentuate her rapture blue eyes and impassive stare. Slowly, her mouth twisted into a smile as though she were welcoming prey into a dark embrace.

Joe took the seat opposite and sat in silence, waiting for her to speak. He maintained his stare, not wanting to appear weak in her presence though he had to fight his urge to say something. Heather was sat in the chair by the DVD recorder, Sue positioned by her client.

Joe was desperate to know why she had asked for him. She didn't keep him waiting much longer.

"He admired you, you know."

"Who did?" Joe replied.

"Stark. He admired your drive and determination."

Joe chuckled. "And you know this how? It's not like he'll have told you."

"We know," Rebecca responded confidently. "We know everything. We know that you live in Fenit, that you used to work for The Daily Eire and that your ex-girlfriend is called Emma."

Joe leaned back in his chair, as though trying to distance himself from her comments. "You could have got that from Google. That's hardly supporting your claim to being holders of great epistemology."

"What does that mean?" Rebecca queried.

"It means knowledge," Joe responded with a wry smile. "Apologies, I've been accused of using big words in the past that people can't understand. Journalistic habits die hard."

"Amusing," Rebecca countered. "How about we know you were one of the last people to see Obadiah Stark alive, made contact with The Brethren and that your bank account has in it, as of yesterday, one hundred and forty five euros."

Joe stared back at Rebecca. "Okay, you have my attention."

Heather leaned forward. "Why did you want to speak to this man," she asked impatiently.

Rebecca returned her gaze with a silent, unblinking stare.

Heather nodded in understanding. "Okay, Mr O'Connell. Ask her?"

"Why did you want to speak to me?" Joe repeated.

"Because you're part of the plan."

"What plan?" Heather asked. Again, Rebecca gave her nothing.

Heather nodded towards Joe. "What plan?

"The plan to spread Obadiah's word."

"And what was his word?" Joe echoed as instructed.

"That by pushing boundaries, one usually finds the truth."

"Tell us about the tattoo?" Heather asked and Joe restated.

"It reminds us that we're family. That his words were not spoken but realised."

"You mean killing people?" Joe interjected.

"Oooo, we were told you were smart. Clever boy."

"By whom?" Heather asked. With another response of silence, Joe repeated the question.

"Our voice… our salvation."

"Does this messiah have a name?"

"Yes."

"And it is?"

Rebecca made a tut-tut noise. "Joe, you were doing so well and you had to go and spoil it repeating a stupid question you know I won't answer."

"Okay, I'm sorry," Joe said with genuine sincerity. Having had a taste, he wanted more and didn't know how much longer Heather would tolerate her games.

"How many people have you killed?"

"Me personally, just Susan," Rebecca gloated. "Collectively, seven."

"Seven people," Joe repeated with slight surprise. "How come no one's heard about this?"

"Why would you? Kill someone publicly, the world will know. Kill someone subtly, quietly… well, let's just say some people the world won't miss."

"How many of you are there?" Heather instructed Joe to ask.

"There were 27, now there's 25."

"The other two being Susan and yourself?" Joe calculated.

"Correct. Great achievement is often only attained through

sacrifice. We gave ourselves in order for his word to be heard and for you to be acquired."

"Why?"

"Because we can… because the world is drowning in putrefaction. Chaos. Depravity. A message needs to be sent for all to see. A message etched in the blood of the chosen. A warning you'll help us deliver."

Joe looked at Heather who seemed to understand and nodded reluctantly. "And what makes you think I'll have anything to do with your game?" He asked.

"Because you have no choice," Rebecca said assertively. "You're already playing, you just don't realise it."

Joe thought before he spoke, knowing that Heather would likely have a conniption fit for him not having mentioned what he was about to say to her first.

"What's in your back between your shoulder blades?" Heather shot Joe a look that could have melted adamantium.

Rebecca smiled knowingly. "Ah, you spotted that, did you? It's insurance."

"What are you talking about?" Heather demanded.

The solicitor began fidgeting uncomfortably in her seat, clearly ignorant as to what was going on.

"I noticed on one of the photos that there appeared to be something on, or rather in, her back," Joe said, pausing for dramatic effect.

"And you failed to mention this earlier, why?"

Joe considered his answer, never once removing his gaze

from Rebecca. "You need to have it removed and examined."

Heather stood and moved behind the suspect, gently pulling down the top of her t-shirt. Rebecca made no attempt to stop her. "I think we're done here," she announced, absentmindedly releasing Rebeca's top. "I think you should wait outside, Mr O'Connell."

Joe nodded, taking one last look at Rebecca before rising from his chair and making his way out of the room.

Heather's dark expression followed him as he left before turning back to her suspect.

"So, you feel like telling me about the MacGyver'd device under your skin?"

Rebecca firmed her lips and remained silent. "That's what I thought," Heather said.

Heather had marched from the interview room, angry and frustrated.

Now, watching Rebecca via the monitors, she began to feel the tendrils of uncertainty creeping around her mind, trying to take hold. She refused to let them. This case was too important and had just literally blown up to monumental proportions right before her.

"What the fuck was that all about?" Her tone was angry and scared at the enormity of what they had just learnt. As though realising she sounded like she wasn't in control, she slowly ran her hands threw her black hair and took a deep breath.

Joe moved to rest on the edge of the table, his back to the mirror. "I have no idea. She knows things no one should know about that night."

"No, I mean the fucking bombshell about the what-ever-the-hell-it-is sown into her back."

"I'm sorry," Joe said sincerely. "I should have told you about it before."

"You're goddamn right you should have!" Heather said. "I've got the doctor in there right now trying to work out how we can remove it without infringing her fucking civil liberties."

"They'll know where she was taken following her arrest," Joe said under his breath as though working through a problem. "So its use as a kind of GPS is redundant. I have a feeling it functions as something else instead."

"Like what?" Heather asked.

"I have no idea," Joe replied in frustration.

Heather looked around the room as though someone would fashion a suitable explanation. When none was forthcoming, she turned her attention back to Joe.

"And who are these Brethren she mentioned? Not The Brethren lawyers who support the unjust or whatever their log line is these days?"

"I take it you're not a fan?"

"Am I bollocks!"

"I'll tell you about that in private," Joe said cautiously, casting a quick glance at Alex who responded with an amazing resting bitch face. "What is important is that she admitted to seven murders. Do you know about them?"

Heather bit her bottom lip as she mumbled her response. "No. But I'll get someone on doing a search for any missing persons. We might get lucky… I can't imagine she's going to give us names."

"I wouldn't count on it," Joe replied. "And you might have bigger problems. If I had to hazard a guess, I'd say she is part of a cult."

"And how did you come to that conclusion, Clouseau?"

"Because she more or less admitted it," Joe snapped back.

"Either that or she's in a girl band."

Heather sighed wearily at his sarcasm.

"Look, she spoke of them in plural," Joe continued. "She implied they had a leader, she said there were 25 of them. They seem to be influenced by the philosophies of Obadiah Stark and I imagine, given what she knew about my bank account, have a lot of power or inferred power at the very least. She already stated they've killed seven people."

"How incompetent do you think we are," Alex snapped. "Don't you think we'd have known if people suddenly started turning up mutilated?"

"Who says they were mutilated?" Joe challenged. "Who says they turned up at all? It's not without precedent. The Colonial Parkway Killer, a 23 mile stretch of road in Virginia plagued by a series of unsolved murders. The Connecticut River Valley Killer who over ten years murdered at least seven women, not all of whom were discovered immediately. The Night Stalker, not Richard Ramirez but his predecessor, who potentially claimed the lives of eight victims and was later identified as also being the East Area Rapist… same killer, no suspect. Serial killers can go about their business for a long time before anyone even realises that the killings are by the same person. And if he, or they, were killing people no one would necessarily miss as she said, then why would you know about it?"

"But Stark was a lunatic," Heather countered. "Why on earth would anyone want to follow his outlook on life?"

"Obadiah was a smart man," Joe considered. "People who join a cult tend to be lost in life, looking for something that will speak to them on a personal level. If those individuals are particularly vulnerable, someone could get them to believe in any doctrine he, or she, wished. Convince a little man that he's serving some great cause and he'll do anything for you."

"Kill for you?"

"Absolutely," Joe responded. "He'll torture people, mutilate people… and he'll do it with a smile."

"Or she will," Heather corrected.

"Indeed," Joe said with a smile of his own."There will always be leaders and followers, Detective. That's the way of the world. This is just that conceit at its most basic, animalistic understanding."

Heather stood still, seemingly enthralled by Joe's words. "Okay, Mr O'Connell. You know this man, or knew him. If any of this is remotely true, what can we expect?"

Joe grimaced before he spoke. "I'm not sure. We need to speak to someone who understands religion, maybe someone from a university who can explain casts, beliefs, devotion, that sort of thing. One thing I am certain of though is that we can expect things to get worse before they get better… a lot worse."

The incident room was a hive of activity as Heather walked into the room, closely followed by Alex and Joe behind them.

The noise quickly settled to a low hum as the officers stopped what they were doing and turned their attention to Heather. She looked around the room before beginning.

"So, rumour control, here are the facts. A woman was arrested last night under suspicion of murder, the victim one 28 year-old Susan Claire Bradley. Susan was reported missing three years ago. The suspect, Rebecca Sill, claims that she was instructed to carry out the murder by an unknown individual. It is clear that this crime is about exposure. The victim was deliberately mutilated in order to send a message, the purpose of which currently also remains unknown. What we do know is that this was personal - personal for the perpetrator of the crime and personal in regards to the message it was intended to send."

Heather glanced round at Joe who stood to her right. "Many of you will know Joe O'Connell. The suspect stated that she would only convey information relating to the crime to Mr O'Connell. We remain uncertain as to her motives for this, however through Mr O'Connell's cooperation we managed to glean some details which may prove useful."

She looked at him again, with a look of resignation on her face before continuing with a small sigh. "Mr O'Connell will be assisting us in this investigation."

All eyes swung towards Joe as moans of derision rose from the back of the room that were quickly quelled by Heather.

"I appreciate this is unorthodox and may make some of you uncomfortable, however, Mr O'Connell has already provided us with something that may help get us started on the motive behind this murder and more importantly, who might be behind it. So, to begin with I want all our efforts put into researching local cults. Mr O'Connell believes the suspect is part of one, so I want everything you can dig up about historic, local cults, new ones in the last few years, anything in this country that relates to organised religion."

"Religion?" Officer Stout questioned.

"Yes, religion. All cults are registered as religions, so though we run the risk of upsetting a few people who are genuine, spiritual people, we need to look at everything. Specifically focus on anything that seems to have a penchant for Obadiah Stark."

A buzz went round the room.

"As in The Tally Man, Obadiah Stark?" Officer Kerr queried. "Are you saying there's a cult that believes in that psycho?"

"We're not certain." Heather winced as she acknowledged their lack of solid facts. "But it's clear from the tattoos on the suspect's back there's a link. Some of the information she shared with Mr O'Connell gave us reason to believe there may be a group of people who hold him in some esteem, however much that may be repellent to us. I want us looking into missing people cases from the last five years. There may be more victims linked to this case. I want them checked, and checked again"

"People who join cults often leave home unexpectedly, or run away. We may get lucky. And I'd appreciate it if we didn't use the word 'psycho' to describe one of history's worst murderers, thank you very much."

The admonishment left Officer Kerr flushing from the neck upward, his colleagues around him gently mocking his encroaching embarrassment.

"I want all lines of enquiry followed up. Think laterally. If this is a cult and they've been killing people for some time, I want them found and stopped. I'll be asking for extra manpower to help us with the investigation. Obadiah Stark left this country with a wound that remains raw. Many of his victim's families were denied justice for their loved ones and we owe it to them to honour their memories."

Joe smiled at the irony of Heather's comment about the family's being denied justice. *They got their justice and then some*, he considered. He wondered how she would feel about The Brethren's illicit, punishment techniques for serial killers.

She could sense determination growing amongst her fellow officers and was keen to capitalise on it.

"If there's a group of people who think that Obadiah Stark was a role model they wish to build a religion on, I want them found. If there's a group of people who think that they can build on Obadiah Stark's work, I want them stopped. The press will get hold of this eventually and I don't want them sensationalising this crime and giving that bastard Stark any acknowledgement years after his death. He didn't deserve it then, he certainly doesn't deserve it now. The possible link to Obadiah Stark doesn't leave this room. Is that understood?"

A murmur of acknowledgment circled the room as officers stood up and filed out of the room. Heather turned to face Joe, her expression now one of concern.

"Do you really think there're more victims linked to this?"

Joe considered his answer. "I do. I think that someone made it their business to carry on Obadiah Stark's work in the shadows, and in doing so gained a following. Call them sociopaths, obsessives… whatever term you wish to use, the fact remains that the woman in that room killed someone because she refused to kill someone else. That alone has me afraid."

"Afraid of what?" Heather asked gently.

Joe firmed up his lips and gave his head a mournful shake. "Afraid that if one person can kill in the name of Obadiah Stark, imagine what an army of them could do."

'You want sensitive and understanding, stick with the therapist. You want great, headbanging sex, get off the fucking phone and come with me.'

Jennifer Cruise – *Welcome to Temptation*

Lynsey Currie could feel herself becoming more aroused the more she watched her.

She had been in the Bagots Hutton for over an hour before the woman had walked in. Her red hair was dishevelled, her loose fitting shirt and jeans completing the picture of a woman comfortable with her appearance and all augmented by her stunning looks. Lynsey thought she looked like a model on her day off, one who'd decided to forgo designer clothes and just wear whatever had come to hand.

She had moved towards the bar in long strides, glancing over at Lynsey as she walked past her. Returning the smile the redhead had gifted her, she considered her next move. A couple of guys had moved over to stand either side of her almost immediately, most likely attracted by the same things Lynsey was.

After a little flirting and small talk, she had moved with

them over to a sofa in the corner where they had taken up a position either side of her. And that was where she still was. Drinking, laughing and encouraging them, with the occasional glance in Lynsey's direction.

One of the oldest establishments in Dublin, the Bagots was a cross between a stuffy wine bar and a trendy pub. Comfortable sofas stretched along the back walls and artwork adorned the walls that you could purchase if you were so inclined. The fact the bar had been fashioned inside a former underground wine cellar only added to its sense of history and atmosphere.

Lynsey often came here, not just to indulge her debauched lifestyle but to take a break from the intensity of her life. She liked the sense of normality it provided, reminding her that the rest of the world was still marching to the beat of its own, personal solipsistic drum. Sitting here she would look around and find herself feeling what she could only describe as envy. She had chosen to leave her former life behind and join the ranks of Lamont Etchison's cause, fully believing in his mission, yet wondered how different her life could have been if she'd only realised she had been standing at a crossroads at the time. That said, she did find these occasions exhilarating. The uncertainty and trepidation of how it was all going to unfold.

How would they react once they realised her intentions? How would it make them feel?

Lynsey finished her drink and slid the glass along the bar before moving over towards the redhead and her companions. It was a few moments before anyone noticed she was standing there.

"I was wondering if I could join you?" Lynsey asked.

The man to her left, a squat individual with long, greasy hair and poor skin, looked her up and down before speaking in an Irish drawl. "Of course ya can, darlin' "

"I wasn't talking to you," she replied without taking her eyes of the redhead. "I was talking to her."

Squat cast a look at his colleague, a taller man who was casually dressed in jeans and a t-shirt, smelt like whiskey and smiled at what they though was their good fortune.

"Well, you're more than welcome to join us all. There's more than enough room here." He patted the space he had made beside him.

Lynsey looked at him with disappointment. "Typical man. You think because I find her attractive we're going to strip each other naked right here and now and have sex on the floor whilst you watch? You're so predictable."

She turned her attention back to Red. "So, what do you say? Fancy going somewhere else for a drink?"

The redhead smiled and stood up, politely gesturing her way past the men.

"Fucking dykes," Squat said angrily. "So, you were just stringing us along, siting here with your flirty smile and fuck-me eyes?"

"Not at all," Redhead fired back eloquently. "I was having fun, but that's all it was… fun. We weren't all going to be going home together if that's what you were thinking, but nor was I stringing you along. I enjoyed our drink, but this lady is more my cup of tea. Have a nice evening gentlemen."

She turned to face Lynsey, a seductive smile on her face. "So, you have anywhere particular in mind?"

She ran her hands down the sides of her waist and around her bottom before slowly easing her down onto the floor. Lynsey looked the woman in the eyes, gently brushing hair from her face.

They'd popped into a few more pubs on the way back to Lynsey's flat, laughing, dancing and consuming more Sambuca shots than sensible. The redhead, whose name Lynsey now knew was Catriona, had slammed her against the wall before the door to the flat was closed. Merged together, they'd fumbled up the stairs and into the living room before settling onto the floor.

But now, staring into her large, brown eyes, Lynsey realised she felt guilty. The last one hadn't provoked this feeling in her, but perhaps that was because she had proven to be a complete bitch when she'd gotten her home, all cocky and sure of herself. Lynsey certainly hadn't had any issue doing what was required with that one, even if just to shut her up.

She sometimes found it amusing that most people spent their lives trying to avoid thinking about death, seeing only sunny rooms and imagining the presence of a loved one close by, whereas it was now her job to facilitate it.

It hadn't been so hard at first, compartmentalising what she was doing and rationalising that as she was only preparing them, not killing them. But more and more recently, Lynsey had been aware of something unspoken, lying beneath the surface of her self validation. An unspoken disquiet about the part she played. But now she realised what it was that had been slowly growing inside her, corrupting her like a fungus.

Lynsey truly believed in Lamont and the Obadians. She had left her old life behind because it was antiquated and bereft of hope for the future. He had given her purpose, something to strive for and a family to be part of. What was asked of them she hadn't originally seen as crimes but necessary evils, driving their belief towards its epitome.

But now she wasn't so convinced. She had seen things, heard things that now made her question whether the reason she had joined them was the reason she still stayed. Lynsey didn't want the woman in front of her to be part of that mission.

"Are you having second thoughts?" Catriona asked, breaking her reverie.

"No, not about you."

"Good," Catriona said, sliding her hand up the inside of her thigh. "Because I've been dying to do this since I saw you."

They kissed passionately, pulling at each other's clothing and peeling off layers until they were both in their underwear. Catriona stared intently into Lynsey's eyes before slowly moving down, kissing her shoulder, the line of her neck, her elbows. She gently tickled the backs of her knees, eliciting a giggle from Lynsey that she hadn't expected.

She gasped slightly as Catriona worked her way back up, gently caressing her lower stomach with her tongue and then moving onto her breasts, nibbling at her nipples softly through her bra. Her hand slid down to rest between Lynsey's thighs, dragging her fingers lazily around the outside of her knickers before sliding them underneath. Lynsey moaned as she felt her circling around, slowing entering and leaving her in a steady, controlled motion.

She found herself licking her lips repeatedly, uncertain whether it was out of desire or thirst. Catriona's trembling fingers gently teased her towards a precipice as she felt warmth slowly rising from her feet whilst at the same time sinking from her head and settling around her stomach.

Lynsey's whole body shuddered as she climaxed, her breathing coming in short, staccato gasps. Catriona moved her body up until they were face to face.

"You okay?" she asked, hair matted to her brow.

"I am," Lynsey replied, her breathing exaggerated. "You've obviously done that before," she joked.

"Hmmm, maybe once or twice," Catriona replied with a coy smile.

Lynsey suddenly found herself overcome with sadness at what she knew she had to do. She knew her suffering would be legendary if she refused. "What's wrong?" Catriona asked, gently caressing her face.

Pushing her hand away, Lynsey stood up and grabbed her trousers, putting them back on as she walked towards the kitchen.

She grabbed a cigarette from the packet on the workbench and lit it. Catriona rose and moved through the blue haze hanging in the air between them.

"Have I done something to upset you?" she asked sadly.

Lynsey held her gaze, considering her response. "No. It's not you."

"Oh, that's funny. The old 'it's not you, it's me' line. I guess you just got me drunk and brought me here for a good fuck so you could then throw me out having taken what you wanted."

"Don't be silly. It's not like that," Lynsey said wearily. "I just have something on my mind and this was a distraction from it, but now the fantasy's over and reality's back in charge. Some things just can't be avoided."

"Deep," Catriona responded. "So, that's it then. No point in my asking for your number?"

"No," Lynsey said quietly before walking towards the bathroom. Catriona stared at her retreating figure for a few beats before gathering her clothes from the living room floor. "Well, can you at least call me a taxi," she shouted as she sat down on the sofa to put on her jeans.

"You don't need to worry about getting home," Lynsey said from behind her, causing Catriona to jump.

"*Jesus!* Stealth-like much?" she announced, as she pulled on her shirt. "Why, you now going to ask me to stay the night?"

Lynsey shook her head. "I wish I could. And I just wanted to say that I'm sorry."

"Sorry for what?" Catriona asked as she moved around the sofa and stood in front of her.

"For this."

Lynsey raised her right hand and gently cupped her cheek.

She held it there for a moment before bringing up her left hand and jabbing the syringe into Catriona's neck.

She let out a small yelp and slapped her hand where the needle had penetrated.

"I'm so sorry, I truly am," Lynsey said as she moved back a few steps. "I have no choice."

Catriona looked at her with a confused expression before her eyes rolled into the back of her head. Lynsey grabbed her as she collapsed and gently guided her onto the sofa. She lifted up her legs and repositioned her, gently brushing some of the hair from her face for the second time that evening.

She grabbed the phone from the table and speed-dialled the only number stored. A female voice answered after the fourth ring.

"It's me. Tell Lamont it's done."

"Any problems?" asked the voice.

"No," Lynsey responded, hoping the uncertainty wasn't apparent in her voice. "No problems."

'It has been said time heals all wounds. I do not agree. The wounds remain. In time, the mind protecting its sanity covers them with scar tissue and the pain lessens, but it's never gone.'

Rose Kennedy

JOE SHUFFLED ABOUT ON THE SOFA TRYING TO GET comfortable, fiddling with the satchel beside him.

He felt ill at ease. Back when he had been an investigative journalist at *The Daily Eire*, this would have been a fairly routine day for him. Speaking to family members who had lost loved ones or to those suspected of a crime had been where he had felt most relaxed. But now sat opposite the parents of Susan Claire Bradley, he considered he would rather be back in the room with Obadiah Stark.

Distanced from his former job, he realised how intrusive it was to enter peoples' homes to pry information from them. Heather had granted him permission to speak to Susan's parents, but expressly stipulated that he relay anything he learnt back to her. They had lengthened his leash, but Heather still had a tight hold on it to ensure that if he went for a shit, she would be watching to make certain he picked it up.

Martina Bradley looked at least ten years older than her actual 41 years of age. Her light brown hair was pulled back into a tight ponytail that only served to emphasis the drawn look around her hazel eyes that looked as though they'd never had a break from crying.

Dressed conservatively in a grey jumper and long, navy blue skirt she had the appearance of someone once attractive but whom life had worn away like water erodes a cliff-face.You could see what had once been there, but only as an afterimage.

Her husband Stephen was almost the exact opposite. Handsome and well built, he had the appearance of a former rugby player who had learned that size wasn't everything but still maintained his gym membership. At least six feet tall, his black hair was perfectly styled across his forehead as though ready for a photograph. Dressed in jeans and a t-shirt, he was barefoot and looked as though he was projecting strength rather than believing it. Only his hand on her shoulder as they sat together belied the fact that he was as anxious as her about the purpose of Joe's visit.

"Why don't you make Mr O'Connell some tea, love," Stephen asked his wife.

"No, thank you. I'm fine," Joe replied, gesturing for Martina to sit back down. "I realise this must be hard for you both. Please allow me to offer my condolences."

They nodded in acknowledgement of his sentiment. "I'll try and keep this brief, but I was wondering if you could tell me a little about Susan before she disappeared."

Martina glanced up at her husband as though seeking permission to speak. He nodded his consent.

"She was a quiet girl. Gentle… very timid and shy. She didn't really have friends and spent most of her time in her room. She'd just left university and was hoping to be a solicitor. Very bright our Susan… very bright." Her voice tailed off to barely a whisper.

Joe waited a moment before he spoke. "Did she offer any indication that something was bothering her prior to her disappearance?"

"She didn't disappear, Mr O'Connell," Stephen interjected. "She was taken. Seduced by those… people… by that woman. She saw a vulnerable girl and convinced her of God knows what. Susan started staying out late, going to people's houses for dinner or staying with people for the weekend, talking about things we didn't understand…"

"Had there been any trouble between you all?" Joe asked.

"What are you implying? That we drove her away? That this is all our fault?"

"No," Joe assured him in the most sincere voice he had. "Absolutely not. I'm simply trying to establish her motivation to join the people she ended up with."

Martina gently wiped at the tears welling in her eyes. "Do you know who they were, Mr O'Connell? It was a cult, wasn't it?"

"The police are looking into it, Mrs Bradley," Joe answered, evading the question.

"It's okay," she replied. "I know it was. The things she used to say, about how they had made her feel like she had a purpose and that they'd opened up her mind to her true potential. Maybe if we'd been better parents… looked after her more then she wouldn't have felt as though some strangers could give her what her family couldn't."

"You can't blame yourself. These people are very clever and see vulnerabilities, uncertainty, and indifference as opportunities to exploit. For those people who feel overwhelmed by life's ambiguity, religion can offer an instant, simplistic solution to life's problems. I can see the appeal. If you've ever been in that place emotionally where you wonder what the point is and if you offer anything to the world… if you were to die, whether anyone even notice, then these kinds of faiths can seem like the answer to all of your problems."

Neither of them spoke and simply stared at Joe with expressions desperate for answers.

"You said there was a woman," he asked to plaster over the uncomfortable silence. "Do you know who she was?"

Martina shook her head. "No, we'd never seen her before. As I said, Susan had no real friends. But suddenly this woman started calling round to see Susan at all hours, sometimes in the middle of the night. Her name was… Justine. Yes, Susan called her that once I think. She was always pleasant, but a little… off. Something just wasn't right about her. It wasn't that she was opinionated, but more that she was forthright."

"About what?"

"About everything. Her sexuality, her life… she joined us for dinner once and started talking about how the human race was facing an epoch that would force it to confront its own failings. It was all about how her group had taken on board philosophies of someone who had understood how mankind was in need of a teacher, to show them how pointless our existence really was and how we needed to be freed from it. Scary stuff, but Susan just sat there nodding in agreement as though she'd believed these things all her life. Our daughter became a complete stranger to us just sat around a dinner table, Mr O'Connell. How do you deal with that?"

Joe paused considerately before speaking. "I don't know. This Justine, did you get a surname?"

"No," Martina replied. "Just her first name."

"What about her appearance? What did she look like?"

"She was tall. Striking eyes, really blue but had an intense stare as though trying to read your mind. Well spoken… not Irish. Northern England I think."

Joe had grabbed a note pad from his satchel and was making notes."That's really useful, Mrs Bradley. One more thing, did Susan ever happen to mention where these people were based she was spending time with?"

"No, nothing at all. You have to remember, Mr O'Connell that towards the end she hardly spoke to us except when we were arguing or she was trying to convert us to her way of thinking. We tried to reason with her on the odd occasion she rang us after she'd first left. I used to say to Stephen that she was having doubts and that her calls were her way of trying to reach out to us, but he was never convinced. And it turns out she wasn't. Maybe she was just checking to see if we were okay… I like to think so. But when she stopped calling, because we had no idea where she had gone, we weren't able to speak to her again. We reported her as a missing person to the Gardaí but they never found any indication as to where she'd gone.

"They often alluded to the fact that we had to accept the possibility that she was dead, but I never believed it… well, not until now. I don't know what was worse, believing she was dead all this time or now knowing that she was alive and choosing to ignore us. I weep for the daughter I lost, Mr O'Connell, the girl who walked out the door that day, I have no idea who she was. Certainly not the daughter who I'd raised, loved and cared for all her life.

"They say when you lose a parent you lose your past and when you lose a child you lose your future. And it's true. I know now why there is no word for the loss of a child. How can there be? Lose a husband and you're a widow, lose a parent and you're an orphan… lose a child and you're what? Bereft? And yet, and I know this may sound cold and heartless as no parent should ever outlive their own child, but she was already lost to us. The grief we felt before was tempered with hope that one day she might come back to us. But now, knowing we'll never see her again, the grief is just boundless. I just hope she was happy with the life she had chosen. Was she? Was she happy?"

Joe smiled sadly. "I don't know. I just know the Gardaí will do all they can to find these people. And so will I, I promise."

They both nodded their gratitude at his words, even though Joe could see they didn't quite believe they would ever have closure.

"The person they arrested for her murder," Martina interjected. "Did they say why they did it?"

"No," he replied with a lie. "They haven't really said that much."

"Oh," she said softly. "I was just wondering, you know? I thought maybe if there was a reason it might help."

"They will find who did this," Joe said. He actually found himself believing it. He certainly knew he was going to do everything in his power to help them catch whoever was trying to take the place of Obadiah Stark.

"Thank you," Martina replied, reaching over to grab her husband's hand and squeezing it tight.

Joe rose and nodded his gratitude to them both for their time. As he made his way towards the front door he noticed Martina's face had imperceptibly softened at his assurance, the faintest smile touching her lips.

He left the house and made his way back towards the car, lighting a cigarette as he went. Throwing his bag on the passenger side seat, he closed the door and leaned back against the vehicle, forcefully exhaling a billowing plume of smoke from his nose.

He needed to know more about this cult and who this woman was. Not only because he had found himself inadvertently embroiled in a murder investigation, but because they were using the name of a man who Joe's obsession with had virtually ruined his life. He found himself breathing heavily as the fluttering he felt in his stomach began to turn into full-blown panic.

Closing his eyes, Joe remembered the mindfulness techniques he had been show by his psychologist for when he found himself feeling anxious. He forcibly slowed his breathing and closed his eyes, taking note of his surroundings and sounds around him. He concentrated on the ground beneath his feet, the cold on his skin and distant sounds of traffic on the main road. As he felt his breathing slow he opened his eyes again, noticing he had flicked his cigarette away without realising.

He refused to let fear ruin his life. Stark had already done that once before: he'd be fucked if he would let it happen again. What happened now would define him for the rest of his life. If he didn't uncover who was doing all of this in Stark's name, not only would the Gardaí be embarrassed but it would hang like an albatross around Joe's neck for the rest of his life.

And he knew just the person to help him.

'And further still at an unearthly height, one luminary clock against the sky proclaimed the time was neither wrong nor right. I have been one acquainted with the night.'

Robert Frost

FEBRUARY 20TH 23:14

UNKNOWN LOCATION IRELAND

CATRIONA HAMILTON AWOKE IN A PLACE FAR FROM
familiar.

A strong smell of chlorine forced her to wrinkle her nose
up in protest as she blinked away the lethargy and shook
herself into an alert state. Even in the low light she noticed
the source of the odour was the two large bottles of bleach
sat on the table in front of her. Towels and gauze swabs
littered the surface along with a large bowl and a pair of
leather gloves. Further along there was a selection of
knives and other instruments she didn't recognise. The
sight of those items alone had her hyperventilating.

Her mind fought against what it was telling her was about
to happen as a range of emotions suddenly burst from her
simultaneously. Fear, loneliness, denial, all merged together,
her body wanting to vocalise them all at once in a
desperate antiphon.

The tremors working their way around her body were like
internal earthquakes. They would rise in ripples and then

explode through her, causing her teeth to chatter and her muscles to seize. Her life had turned upside down in the space of a few hours. One moment she had been oblivious to the rest of the world as she danced and had made love to Lynsey. Now, she was hogtied to a chair with her legs kicking rhythmically to the beat of the spasms as she fought an urge to vomit. The fact that she was bound to a chair assured her with the uttermost certainty that the only reason she was here was to suffer.

Spasms seemed to slam from her body as waves of fear suddenly crashed over her in rhythmic beats, her heart seemingly insistent on repeating its discordant thumping until she was apoplectic with dread.

After what seemed like an eternity, the spasms wracking her body slowly subsided. Cramp-like pain washed over her as her body forced itself to relax after being tense for so long. Her breathing became more regulated and her heart discontinued its battle to burst loose from her chest. She thought she knew how John Hurt's character must have felt in Alien as his parasitic copilot decided to birth itself unbidden.

Catriona glanced around the room, able to recognise she was in a basement of some kind. It was warm but not uncomfortably so. She looked down over her body and saw rope binding her tightly to the chair she was occupying. She could stretch out her legs at the knee and flex her hands at the wrist, but aside from that she was fixed tightly. She felt something wet beneath her bare feet, immediately thinking she must have wet herself during her moment of panic but realised it was most likely sweat that had pooled beneath her, as her clothes were wringing wet.

The dampness did little to subdue the shaking she was experiencing or the cold sensation wrapping her body.

Catriona knew however, that the cold dread she felt also had something to do with the figure she could now make out standing in the corner of the room. She immediately realised that whoever it was before her was far from benign and likely intent on doing her harm. She could tell he was quite a large man, yet when he spoke his voice was unnaturally calm and had a childlike lilt to it.

"Don't scream," the man asked. "If you make even one noise I will have to ensure you are hurt. Are we clear?"

She found herself nodding dumbly in response, as her mind tried to work out if any of this was actually real. The million questions racing through her mind simply collided and splintered into an indecipherable jumble of useless phrases and letters.

Catriona tried to speak but found she had no voice, fear having removed all of her strength and leaving her vocal cords paralysed. After a few moments of croaking, she managed to whisper out a question in a trembling manner.

"Where am I?"

"Somewhere where devotion and conviction align, my dear," the man replied. "By the way, forgive my manners. Etchison. Lamont Etchison."

"What do you want with me?" Catriona whispered hoarsely.

"I want to show you that you're special. You've been chosen to further a belief that began with one individual a long time ago and is now being perpetuated by us."

"And who are you?"

"A family. Not in the literal sense you understand, but in the spiritual. You're to be a messenger to those who still believe that honesty comes painlessly. Mankind still believes that growth of the human spirit is the end of human existence. I mean to show them that in order to grow we need to avail ourselves of the legitimate shortcuts that exist around us. Many people cheat on their journey to understand themselves and what they're capable of.

"Consider reading the synopsis of a good book. You can understand the book in its entirety from a good synopsis without ever opening it up. That's not cheating, but merely taking advantage of the *legitimate* shortcuts available to you. But so many people in life cheat on their understanding of how things are meant to be. They don't read the synopsis, they look on Wikipedia or ask someone else to interpret it for them and then the message gets lost. It may save time in the long run, and you may even understand the rudimentary basics of the story, but you won't have attained essential knowledge from the source material. You will have simply gained a misrepresentation of the truth. And that's why you're here. To provide those who believe that the message died with Obadiah Stark with an understanding that they have been relying on false idols for their information and that we are the source material… the synopsis if you will."

"Where's Lynsey?" Catriona asked.

"Somewhere," Lamont replied vaguely. "She has done her part in bringing you to us. What happens next is another's responsibility."

Catriona choked on the tears that were now freely flowing

down her face. "Why are you doing this to me?"

"I told you, you're here to convey a message to those who think the world is uniform and exact. The politicians, government and bleeding hearts who seem to think they control the world and all that occurs within it. They are only part of a masquerade, one that has been underway for more than one hundred years, orchestrated by individuals more powerful than you could imagine. It is my job to demonstrate that the world is a labyrinth and that the people in it are lost. We are here to show them the way."

"The route to enlightenment may seem deceptively apparent, but the destination is unknown. Obadiah Stark knew this and tried to light the way, but was persecuted by those who prefer to remain comfortable in their own ignorance. The secrets he tried to unveil remain hidden. It has fallen to us to continue his work, to unlock those mysteries and walk those unknown corridors, illuminating that final solution. Your sacrifice will take us one step closer."

"Please… let me go," Catriona begged.

"Ah, the sweet lament of supplication. It never gets old and always remains exquisite."

Lamont turned his back to her and walked towards the door at the end of the room. Opening it, she overheard him uttering something to whoever was standing outside. He stood in the doorway, allowing Catriona to see light shining through the spaces around his body, teasing her with the anguish of freedom as though the light itself was beckoning her to see where her future had once existed but was now a fading reality.

After a few moments, Lamont stepped aside to allow a woman into the room.

"This is Justine. She is one of The Branch Obadians most devoted. She truly believes in the cause and the words that Obadiah spoke during his time *in extremis*. In order to demonstrate to the world the power of our message, we have taken on responsibility for continuing the message that he shared over the course of his 27 martyrs. We will attain the 27; you will be our eighth. Where once you thought of pain as a shadow, it has a face. Justine will show it to you."

Catriona shook with fear, pleading with Lamont. "Please, just let me go. I won't tell anyone anything… I swear."

He smiled and gestured in impatience towards Justine, who nodded her understanding and stepped over to the table. She slowly pulled on the leather gloves, intertwining her fingers to flatten them down between the webs.

"Oh my god!" Catriona shouted out between sobs. "Help me, somebody please help me!"

Lamont moved to the door, turning to her as he left. "Unbearable, isn't it, the waiting, the anticipation? Justine will show you the secret desires hiding at the centre of the world, the ones we keep in those shuttered and dank places. But eventually, unbidden, they make their way to the surface and yearn to be free. They crave to be heard and their music is like knives carving through flesh. It's only quiet now but if you listen closely when Justine begins her work the volume will increase and you will be able to press your wretched face into its dark heart and drink deep of its message. Thank you Catriona, for giving yourself to The Branch Obadians."

The door clicked shut behind him, leaving the only sounds remaining in the room Catriona's weeping and Justine's fevered breathing as she stepped towards her subject.

"Please," she begged. "Don't hurt me."

Justine smiled sympathetically and moved the knife with terrifying fluidity across her abdomen. Catriona cried out in pain as it viciously shredded her stomach again and again.

Justine moved behind her, wiping the blood casually from her face. Catriona felt fingers moving around the top of her neck and her spine as though looking for something. She felt the fingers pausing in a location at the top of her spine as though they'd found what they'd been looking for. The initial stab was brutal, the pain only temporary as the knife severed some of the nerves. She didn't feel the knife work its way past her muscle and tissue, penetrating deeper into her body. Warm blood ran down her right arm and dripped onto the floor.

She felt fingers probing her back again and moaned out a weak challenge for Justine to stop. Once again, her fingers seemed to pause over a specific location as she plunged the knife deep between her vertebrae. The pain was unbearable but Catriona found she was no longer able to cry out. Her mouth moved like a fish taking in water but nothing emanated from inside.

The last thing she felt were the warm tears running down her face as the room began to slip into darkness.

The last sound she heard was Justine chuckling under her breath.

'The beginning of knowledge is the discovery of something we do not understand.'

Frank Herbert

THE CITY THRUMMED WITH ENERGY AS JOE MADE HIS WAY
up Baggot Street.

He walked past Searsons and the Waterloo, two of the
pubs that made up the infamous 'Baggot Mile', a popular
pub-crawl for stag dos and hen nights. It was also the
preferred crawl for the Twelve Pubs of Christmas,
something he had done on many an occasion. He made a
mental note to pop into one of them when he was done
this morning.

The sun was always over the yardarm somewhere.

Joe never got tired of Dublin. They say living in a city all
your life ensures that the most beautiful of surroundings
become the most mundane of characteristics. He didn't
agree. James Joyce had a point when he'd written that
'history is a nightmare from which I am trying to wake'.

It was certainly the case for Joe with everything that had

gone on over the past few years. The country he loved had become the source of his life's darkest moments, yet it held the same appeal to him that it always had. Hope sprang from every pore and crevice, reminding him of a time when Ireland was a bleak and oppressed country that chose not to be governed and would forge its own destiny. Neither a dead serial killer nor a century old cabal was going to dictate his future. It was his to choose and lose at his sufferance.

Wandering past Patrick Kavanagh's statue, Joe turned up the collar of his jacket to the biting cold wind that had risen up from nowhere. The sun was fighting to make its presence known, but he feared it was going to lose this round.

He found himself wondering for the umpteenth time whether the building he was walking past was the one Sinéad Marie Bernadette O'Connor had owned, before turning onto Haddington Road and making his way up the stairs to number 53.

He rang the intercom and waited only a few moments before a voice with a southern English accent came through the speaker.

"Who is it?"

"You can see who it is, Sim! Open the door."

There was an audible tut before the intercom went silent. Ten seconds later he heard the door unlock with a click and a buzz. Joe pressed it closed behind him and slowly made his way up the flight of stairs towards Sim's flat. The walls were decorated with peeling anaglypta wallpaper and areas of mould where damp had taken the next evolutionary leap. Rotten bannisters and dirty carpet gave off the strong impression that the upkeep of this building was minimal, if not non-existent.

Anyone walking in would probably feel inclined to turn around and leave. And that was the point. Sim was suspicious to the point of being almost unsociable.

It had taken him four of his twelve years with *The Daily Eire* to even begin gaining her trust. He could understand it from a certain perspective—her work as a data analyst and hacker meant she wasn't necessary at the top of the authority's Christmas list. After a few run-ins with them, Sim had preferred to keep her skills hidden from the world. It was those skills Joe needed today.

He reached the top of the stairs and knocked twice on the dirty cream door in front of him. It snapped open as far as the security chain would allow, dreadlocked blonde hair and inquisitive brown eyes presenting themselves between the gap. She always reminded him of a cat - pert nose, wide eyes and as watchful and alert as any predator.

"Come on Sim, who else is it going to be?"

The door slammed shut and was followed by the sound of chains being unhooked and locks being slid across. He smiled at her propensity for security, knowing that it was simply overkill. She had enough hidden infrared sensors and cameras to put the Impossible Mission team to shame.

As she led Joe to the living room, he smiled knowingly at the austere and perfectly organised space before him. Sim had deliberately left the remainder of the building to act as a direct contrast to her living space as she not only thought the entrance acted as a deterrent for visitors but that it was also a facsimile of her mind - outer layers of messy, inner layers of orchestrated perfection.

As he followed her, he saw only symmetry. Picture frames, ornaments, clocks. All the same rectangular shape, all positioned specifically. Brown wooden doors, stained brown wooden floors with matching rugs, brown settee, a vase full of burgundy chocolate dahlia flowers and brown blinds shuttered at the windows. Only the huge bank of high specification computer screens against the back wall of the living room looked out of place.

The tech was enough to make Gene Hackman in *Enemy of the State* envious. PCs, eavesdropping equipment, cloning devices littered both of the workspaces Sim had erected between her array of monitors.

"So, what do you want, Joe?" she asked.

"Straight to business, eh? Some things never change," he replied jocularly.

"I don't have time for small talk, I'm busy."

"Okay," Joe said, slightly hurt by her steely demeanour. "I need you to look into someone for me. I recently got involved in a case, much to my surprise and want to do a little digging myself."

"The Bradley murder," Sim stated.

"Yeah," Joe said, surprised. "How do you know that?"

She looked at him with an exasperated glare and gestured around the room. "I'm unsociable, not retarded. What do you think all of this is for? The Next Boxing Day sales? I know everything that goes on."

"Well, in that case," Joe continued. "You should be able to find something out about this lady, Rebecca Sill."

Sim span round in her chair and typed the name into the

keyboard. "What do you want? Basic demographics or skeletons so deep in your closet I know the first time they took a piss?"

"First piss will be good."

"Who is she?" Sim asked without facing him.

"Murder suspect," Joe replied. "Actually, scratch that. Make that murderer. She already confessed to it."

"And why the interest?"

"Because I think she's part of a cult that have been doing this for a while and who have an unhealthy obsession with Obadiah Stark."

Sim stopped typing and turned around. "Oh."

"Yeah," Joe said. "*Oh*, indeed."

"I know you'll get annoyed at me asking this," she said as she turned back to her keyboard. "But should you be getting involved in this?"

"What do you mean?"

"I mean anything that remotely relates to Obadiah Stark?" Sim turned to Joe again, this time looking concerned. "You know the number he did on you last time. I mean you went all Will Graham."

Joe put down the sculpted figurine of a faceless woman holding a baby and let out a soft chuckle. "He was a psychological profiler Sim, a fictional one at that. I'm a journalist... well, *was* a journalist."

"My point," Sim said with exasperation. "Is that he did a number on you and stuck around in your head. Think about it. You were held captive by an insidious organisation of Machiavellian proportions, seated opposite the world's most notorious serial killer, had already uncovered a huge conspiracy surrounding his 'execution' and oh yeah, had been set up by your girlfriend. Am I missing anything?"

"She wasn't my girlfriend," Joe replied matter-of-factly.

"Fuck-buddy, then," Sim fired back. "But whatever she was, you were put through the ringer sunshine, expecting to die, threatened with extinction if you ever uttered a word about what you'd seen and heard. And here you are, asking questions about a murderer who may have connections to a cult that follows Obadiah Stark. *Follows* Obadiah Stark! Doesn't any of this scream to you 'what the fuck?'"

"It says to me less 'what the fuck' and more 'hmmm, intriguing'."

"You're a fucking idiot," Sim stated and began banging furiously on her keyboard. "And you're going to get yourself killed. I don't even know why I'm doing this for you."

Joe bent down and gave her a hug around the chair. "Because you love me."

"Get the fuck off," she replied, shrugging him away partly in annoyance. "Anyway, here you go."

Sim indicated to the chair beside her. Joe sat down and shuffled it closer.

"Okay, Rebecca Sill, daughter of Margaret and Ronnie. 32, one sibling, no children. Grew up in the North East of England, moved to Northern Ireland when she was twelve."

Her ability to find information such as this always amazed Joe. He knew little about the Internet and its scary little brother the Darknet, which he knew Sim used frequently to find out all sorts, so to him, it was the technological equivalent of discovering fire for the first time. Pinging out emails was the pinnacle of his information technology skills.

"Miss Sill bounced around from job to job until she started work at Globoforce in 2004 where she remained until 2009 when she just left and that's the last anyone heard from her. Her family reported her missing to the Gardaí but nothing was ever turned up and she remained off the grid until she turns up having murdered one Susan Bradley the other night."

"Globoforce?" Joe asked.

"They're some sort of provider of social recognition software that aims to 'provide powerful tools and proven methodology to identify key talent and transform your company'… or some shit like that. Basically, they're into encouraging companies to engage with their employees and believe that staff are more productive if they get recognition for what they do. Fortune Magazine named them one of the best places to work in 2013."

"I'll have to get my application in," Joe said glibly. "So, where did she go after that?"

"Not a clue, however, hang on a sec…"

Sim tapped away furiously on the keyboard before leaning back in her chair with a proud look on her face. "Okay, I've found something on your Obadiah crazies. There are some groups on the Darknet who love your boyfriend and think he was the dog's bollocks. One group that has a particular *je ne sais quoi* is the Branch Obadians. No one seems to know when they formed, but it appears they took on many of Stark's philosophies and beliefs of the structured nature of good and evil as their guiding principles. Nothing solid as to their location… a few alleged sightings on Skellig Michael. The Obadians are believed to have originated from a schism in the original 'Family' that followed Stark's teachings, the 'Family' themselves were an offshoot of the Seventh-day Adventist Church."

"Jesus," Joe stated. "This is fucking deep."

"That's religion for you, baby. Anyway, back then they were seemingly known for an emphasis on a holistic understanding of a person, promoting religious liberty, conservative lifestyles, all that free love, happy clappy shit. Later on, it appears the order fractured and moved from lifestyle beliefs to a focus that all life was governed by the Bible's prophecies of a divine judgement as a prelude to a second coming. The Obadians believe this to be Stark rather than Christ."

Joe ran his hands through his hair before running his thumb and forefinger around his beard in a thoughtful manner.

"Rebecca said that Stark was their salvation and that they were sending a message for all to see. 'A message etched in the blood of the chosen' was how she put it, with me helping them deliver it."

"Okay," Sim said curiously.

"So, we can assume she's a member of a cult that'll be made up of like-minded people.'

"Is that what we're calling it?"

"If it looks like a dog and barks like a dog…" Sim shrugged and gestured for him to continue.

"How do you recruit to a cult these days? Charlie Manson used to select people who had emotional and mental health issues, offering them somewhere to call 'home'. Once with him, he used drugs and psychological techniques to break their wills before remaking them in his perceived image. He had no screening mechanism to recruit his followers, so kinda took a leap of faith with the people he trusted to join his Helter Skelter as he used to call it. Nowadays, we're a little more sophisticated. Invite people to a party, poetry reading, concert… something sociable. Love bomb them…"

"Love bombing?" Sim asked incredulously.

"Yeah, love bombing," Joe replied with a smile. "Shower potential recruits with praise and they'll associate being in your company with a good feeling and positive vibes, making them want to come back."

"I'll have to remember that on my next date."

Joe smiled and continued. "Then you dangle a prize in front of them. Money, power, the cure for homosexuality if you're an Aesthetic Realist…"

Sim looked at him suspiciously.

"Oh yeah, apparently it's a disease that requires curing. So that means you're fucked."

"Get stuffed," Sim replied with a smile. "Besides, I'm a Scientologist so I only want answers to the world's mysteries."

"Amusing, " Joe said. "Anyway, do that and back it up with threats, guilt, controlling of identity and information, the whole 'stick and carrot' approach and you can have ready-made recruits willing to do your bidding."

"How do you know all this anyway?"

"I was a reporter, remember. I didn't lose the knack, just my job. And besides, I remember this stuff from the Bridget Crosbie case. She was a member of the Palmarian Catholic Church and was found dead in Wexford. Natural causes, but her family spoke out about the Palmarians saying they'd turned her against them. Cults are all around us Sim, taking people left, right and centre. The only difference is most of them don't have killing as part of their indoctrination. Audits using an e-meter yes, ritualistic murder not so much."

"So, what does this tell us then?" Sim asked as she rose from her chair and headed into the kitchen. Joe followed her at a slow pace. "It tells me that we have a woman who murdered another member of her cult because she was told to, they idolise Obadiah Stark and a woman in custody with a mysterious device sewn into her back."

"But why and who for?" she asked.

"Exactly," Joe conceded. He thought for a moment before speaking. "Keep digging, Sim. See what else you can find out about these Obadians."

"Will do," she said with a nod. "What are you going to do?"

"I'm going to bed and sleeping for a week."

"Well, enjoy and be careful," Sim shouted after him as he made his way towards the front door.

"Careful's my middle name," he replied as the door closed behind him.

"More like careless," she said with a sigh as she moved to the window and stared out over the skyline.

If Sim had looked down, she would have seen a woman watching Joe leaving her flat and follow him down the street.

'Suspicion always haunts the guilty mind.'

William Shakespeare

Lamont had overseen the disposal of Catriona's body.

Unlike Susan, this sacrifice wasn't for public consumption. Her death had been in the interest of momentum, carrying forward Justine's awakening and the Branch's purpose for being.

Catriona hadn't suffered for long, just enough to realise that her being here wasn't as random as she had probably believed. Lamont liked to think Stark would be proud of what they were trying to build; a future for mankind that would no longer be burdened by responsibilities, economic hardships, or political solipsism. He had been tasked to deliver the message Obadiah had started all those years ago. That amongst the cattle there were true visionaries, individuals who saw the world unfettered by opinion or perspective and who realised that for anything worthwhile to be built it has to first be destroyed.

Stark had reportedly only killed 27 people but Lamont

knew it was more than that. An artist doesn't become accustomed to the strokes of his brush without first knowing whether he is skilled with pencils or paint.

Lamont had made it a personal mission to try to discover who those other victims could have been. He had little to go on other than speculation and conjecture, but nevertheless, he knew that if he were to learn how Obadiah had honed his craft they could avoid the mistakes their idol had made. They'd already made good headway, having taken eight in Stark's name. Susan had been a deliberate sacrifice in order to raise their public profile and place O'Connell onto the playing field. Now he was in position, the true game could begin.

Lamont bemoaned the loss of two Obadian members, but those had been his instructions. Rebecca had been a willing martyr to further their message; Susan a tragic loss. He had been truly disappointed to realise she hadn't understood.

Never before had the world been caught up in such raw power and pervasiveness that represented the overtly corrupt political system. The one-percent were leveraging their monopolistic control over every aspect of social media and public opinion, deploying expertise decades in development regarding psychology and turning every facet of public consciousness into a black box process that eluded any accountability and justice.

He knew who was to blame, but those individuals were all key players at the highest levels of power with the ability to influence every man, woman and child on the face of the earth. Some of those people were part of a cabal responsible for the death of Obadiah Stark, right here in Ireland. A facsimile of everything that Lamont despised made up of people who possessed a power they wielded indiscriminately. They would learn of their plans soon enough.

But first things first.

Many would say Lamont was a conspiracy theorist, a nut job who had no credibility, but they knew nothing of his life or who he had been before he'd found solace in the words of Obadiah Stark and by extension, his heir. Now it was his turn to introduce himself to the world.

Joe O'Connell's next move was about to be made for him.

'You can have anything in life if you will sacrifice everything else for it.'

J.M Barrie

THIS IS GETTING COMPLICATED.

Joe looked out of his kitchen window, watching the morning mist drift over the top of the lake causing the boats berthed in the harbour to drift in and out of focus. He took another mouthful of coffee and considered everything he'd learnt so far.

After Starkgate, as he sometimes liked to call it, Joe had made a point of staying away from anything too complicated. Granted, he'd continued an investigation in his own time, but had made certain it was covert. After losing his job and months of therapy to help him manage the anxiety he now experienced, the last thing he wanted was to become embroiled in something dangerous. Yet here he was again, on the precipice of being drawn into a scenario that concerned death, murder and madness in equal measure.

Part of him was screaming to stay away. To not get any further involved and leave the police to handle it. Yet the journalist side of him was always present, subconsciously looking for details others might have missed or clues overlooked.A cult potentially following in the footsteps of The Tally Man was borderline horrific, being in the vicinity of those involved potentially suicidal.

But Joe felt like Obadiah Stark was his responsibility. He had investigated him, studied him, suffered with him and watched him die. He felt he had a duty to those who'd died in his name, irrespective of the hands that had committed the crime.

More than that, they'd requested him. Rebecca had made it explicit that The Branch Obadians wanted him for something, most likely far from good.

A beam of sunlight settled on his eyes, breaking Joe's contemplation. He tried to brush it away like a persistent insect before dropping his cup in the sink and moving into the living room. He flopped onto the settee and had just closed his eyes when the doorbell went.

"For fuck's sake!" Joe whispered under his breath.

He paused for a moment, considering whether or not to ignore it when it rang again.

Sighing loudly, Joe pushed himself up and stood by the window, trying to catch sight of who it was.

A woman he didn't recognise leant against the wall, throwing her arms around herself repeatedly as though cold.

She had bobbed dark hair and a concerned expression on her face, anxiously looking around as though searching for someone or something. For a moment he considered ignoring her, recognising he wasn't in the mood for guests, uninvited or otherwise. But looking at her again, he saw something in her face that made him reconsider.

Not anxiety or urgency. It was more like purpose. She was there for a reason. And the journalist in him was dying to find out why.

Taking a deep, cleansing breath, Joe unlocked the door and presented himself to the woman before him.

"Hi," he said softly.

"Joe O'Connell?" she asked with a certainty that he took as her knowing the answer already.

"I am."

Her shoulders seemed to slump as though she'd just released a heavy burden. "Thank God. I was told where you lived but I wasn't certain it was true."

"Okayyy…" Joe said in a slow drawl. "What can I do for you, Miss…?"

"Maxine. Maxine Groves. And it's more what I can do for you."

Joe considered the woman before him. "I already have double glazing, so sorry I'm not interested."

Maxine smiled nervously. "Funny. No, I'm here about something else."

"And that would be…?"

"The Branch Obadians."

Joe's expression changed from relaxed to concerned. The hairs on the back of his neck stood to attention. He was immediately suspicious that someone claiming to be a member of the organisation Sim had only just identified fortuitously happened to have turned up at his house. Joe internally chastised himself for letting his previous experience affect his judgment. He was a journalist first and foremost. The story always came first, but he would keep his suspicions firmly active in the background.

"You'd better come in," he said, swinging the door open so she could pass.

He gestured to the sofa and leant back against the door, his weight closing it with a soft click.

Like muscle memory, his investigative instincts kicked in. Who, what, where, when, why and how? That was what he needed to know and he needed to know quickly.

Her presence in his home had already changed the atmosphere, as though it shared his unease at the whole situation. Something about her was off.

As he watched her settle back into the sofa, he felt as though she were studying her surroundings, making note of everything in his home. Her black hair and bleached eyes accentuated her attractive face, features Joe found beguiling. At the point he realised he was staring, he cleared his throat and ask if she would like a drink.

"Do you have any beer?" she asked candidly.

"Sorry, no," Joe replied. "I don't drink."

"Anymore," Maxine replied, catching Joe off-guard.

Interesting.

"I'm sorry, have we met before?" he asked curiously. Maxine shook her head, causing hair to fall across her face. As she brushed it back behind her ears, Joe comically thought she looked like an advertisement for shampoo products.

"No, I just know a great deal about you. You're quite the institution. Anyone with an interest in Obadiah Stark or serial killers, in general, has lauded the mighty Joe O'Connell."

Joe paused his pouring of hot water into the two cups holding teabags, holding the kettle in mid-air. She had a soft, well-spoken Irish accent that bordered on being reverent, like Joe's old headmistress.

"I wasn't aware my reputation preceded me," he replied, trying hard not to feel chuffed at her knowledge of him whilst at the same time growing increasingly concerned at the strange woman in his house who seemed to know details she shouldn't.

"Oh, it does," Maxine responded nervously. "Which is why I came to you. Only you can do something with what I'm going to tell you. I know this because you've done it before. Lewis gave you information regarding Stark; you acted upon it, though I'm a little fuzzy on the details."

Now Joe found himself feeling extremely uncomfortable. His anxiety had begun slowly creeping around the fringes of his consciousness, tapping softly at the window of his mind to be let in like Danny in Salem's Lot trying to get to his friend Mark.

He finished making the drinks and reached for his cigarettes. Smoking might mask any tells he might be giving off about his current mental state.

"You knew Dunwall?"

Maxine stood as she moved to his living room window,

gazing wistfully at the harbour below. "I knew Lewis," she confirmed.

Joe blew out a haze of blue smoke. "How?"

There was a pause before she answered. "Another time." Maxine turned from the window to face Joe, her body tensed like a spring waiting to uncoil.

"You're nervous," Joe stated. "Why?"

"Because I shouldn't be here."

Joe stubbed out his cigarette in two attempts and took up a position on the arm of the sofa, all the while staring at Maxine intently. He couldn't help but be intrigued but would be damned if he'd be sucker-punched again. He'd never got over the shame of falling for the 'I'll help you change your flat tire mate whilst secretly wanting to kill you' event orchestrated by The Brethren whilst investigating the Stark case.

"You mentioned the Obadians. How do you know about them?" Joe challenged.

Maxine moved slowly back to the sofa and sat down. She clasped her hands together and began twiddling her thumbs as though considering carefully what she was about to say.

"I know because I *am* one."

Joe sat down next to Maxine, keeping a sizeable gap between them. He was wary of the whole situation and knew he should be on his guard, but his curiosity was screaming.

It might well kill the cat, but I'll happily be a suspect for a while.

"I'm listening," he said assuredly.

Maxine stood again and began to pace around his living room, like a tiger realising it's just been caged.

"You have to appreciate why I'm here," she started, her voice trembling. "The Branch offer purpose, something to believe in… make you feel like you've something to contribute to the world. I guess it's the old 'my family never understood me' cliché, though I think my father would have. The Branch help you see you're not alone, that you can be steadfast in your beliefs."

"They give purpose based on a serial killer's philosophies?" Joe asked, bewildered.

"That's not what it's about," Maxine fired back. "Obadiah Stark understood the way of things. He saw how the world really worked and how one person could make a difference."

Joe laughed in disbelief. "By butchering people. He's not really a good role model to be directing your kids towards, is he? I mean, don't you see how insane it all sounds?"

"What? You're mad because you choose to believe in something outside of the socially accepted norm? It's not killing the Branch believe in, it's his vision. Stark was a very astute individual."

Joe wasn't going to admit it to Maxine, but he agreed with her. Obadiah Stark had been a monster without equal, but a great deal of the erudite statements he was so fond of making held a great deal of truth. Brexit and a controversial businessman in the White House only added to the social discord that Stark had prophetically proclaimed in his interview with the psychologist John Franklin.

"Go on," Joe asked gently. He wanted to keep her focused and talking. More importantly, he wanted to know why she'd turned up at his house.

Maxine took a deep breath. "You've met Rebecca? You've heard what she had to say? Everything that's happened involving you is deliberate. They want you to know that you're the one whom everything is revolving around."

"And the person orchestrating all this is…?" Joe repeated.

"His name is Lamont Etchison. He co-ordinates the Obadians. He's intelligent, cruel, meticulous and obsessed with Obadiah Stark."

"Lamont Etchison," Joe said out loud. "Why do they always have really obsequious names?"

Maxine continued, assuming Joe's question was rhetorical. "The Obadians' fascination with Stark has gone from believing in his cause to creating an homage to it. The '27' they're called. 27 victims to represent…"

"Stark's 27 tally marks," Joe interrupted almost instantly. "Why would someone want to honour a murderer by committing murder?"

Maxine paused for a moment. "It's the fate of glass to break, Joe. The Obadians' message wasn't making a big enough impact, so they decided that if society wouldn't come to them to learn, they would go to them to teach. And their lesson was death."

Joe stood and returned to the kitchen, realising he'd completely forgotten about the tea. Abstractly he stared at the wisps of steam slowly disappearing into the air like forgotten memories. He rubbed his face vigorously, hoping it would force away his fatigue and the magnitude of what he'd just been told.

It only did the former.

"We need to go to the Gardaí with this, tell them what you've told me."

Maxine appeared visibly shaken at the suggestion. "Not a fucking chance!"

She stopped pacing and collapsed to the floor, holding her head in her hands before running them through her hair. As her face rose, Joe saw tears glistening in her eyes, threatening to spill over. "It's just such a fucking mess. And I'm so tired…"

She lay back and closed her eyes. Joe moved to her side and knelt down, putting his arms beneath her back to help her up.

"Woah, you can't stay here."

Standing unsteadily, Maxine glared at Joe with contempt. "You'd throw me out, after everything I've told you? You bastard!"

Joe stepped back his hands in front of him submissively. "Calm down. I'm not throwing you anywhere, I'm just saying you can't stay here. If the Gardaí find out I've had you here and not told them, I'll be shot. If what you say is true and you've just escaped from a serial killing cult and they find out you've been here, I'll literally be shot… or worse. What about your family? Your parents? Shouldn't you go and see them?"

"I don't have any family. My parents are both dead," Maxine said in a low voice.

"Right," he responded awkwardly. "Okay then, I have a friend you can stay with."

Maxine shook her head. "Nope."

Joe picked up his mobile and dialled a number, smiling as he put it to his ears and waited for a response. "Trust me, there's nowhere safer in the country."

On the fourth ring, he heard a sleepy voice answer with the word "What?"

"Sim, it's me. I need you to do me a favour and yes, you'll hate it."

'The moon will guide you through the night with her brightness, but she will always dwell in the darkness, in order to be seen.'

Shannon L. Alder

The winter day was hushed, the only sounds coming through the open windows those of children playing and traffic passing in the distance.

Lamont sat naked in a chair, softly drumming the fingers of his right hand on his thigh. Justine was in the kitchen making them some food, their frenzied afternoon lovemaking leaving them both starving and yet satisfied at the same time. Knowing she'd been responsible for taking that girl's life had made their fucking all the more feverish. He knew she preferred the company of girls, but if she was willing why refuse.

Lamont looked around the room, silently acknowledging its sparse appearance. You couldn't call it dingy, but the large oak trees outside the window created a perpetual state of bleakness. The cream wallpaper was fading and yellowing, most likely due to the previous occupants' smoking habit, the odour of which hung in the air like a perpetual intruder. The single armchair he sat in, an old portable television and a mirror were the only items present, all positioned randomly on a threadbare grey carpet.

He glanced through the kitchen doorway and caught a glimpse of Justine's bare legs as she moved to and fro, his shirt hanging loose and open across her shoulders. A sense of pride washed over him at her accomplishment. Not only had she simply seen to business, but she'd embraced it with a ferocity and an enthusiasm he found enchanting.

Lamont had been tasked with showing society that they'd become lacking in critical thinking skills, not through laziness but by oppression from a system with the power to punish if you didn't give up your individual quest for knowledge. Stark had known this. He had seen that you couldn't fulfil your true spiritual potential unless you defied those who held all the power.

The human race was under an illusion that you either stayed on the production line in order to maintain a level of financial and social security or you defied the system and ended up homeless, living under a bridge in a cardboard box. That was what the governments of the world needed people to believe.

Granted, society required its drone workers, mindless automatons who would be the soldier, the specialist consultant, the nurse and the scientist. But it also needed individuals who were willing to think three dimensionally and consider how to reshape the world around them. The only way to achieve this – and the Obadians true goal – was to increase the number of people with like-minded beliefs. Congregate and educate those willing to break the mould and encourage them to come up with a new shape. Something unexpected. Something original.

Obadiah Stark had known the world was on the verge of a global transformation – politically and socially. The founder of the Obadians had seen it too and had believed all it needed was a gentle push, a crisis that would force others to accept their new world order.

They were starting it here, in the country of his birth. What Obadiah Stark had begun, they would continue. They'd show the world that the words politician and murderer are interchangeable. It just depends on who's doing the naming.

Justine made her way back into the room and sat on the arm of Lamont's chair before handing him his food. She picked at her vegetables with the fork as though they were radioactive.

"I thought you were hungry," Lamont asked softly.

She jabbed at a few more pieces of carrot before placing the plate on the floor beside her. "So did I," she replied coyly. "But seeing you sitting there naked just makes me want to skip dinner and move straight to dessert."

Justine slid off the chair and onto her knees in front of him. She began gently caressing his upper thighs before moving her head towards his crotch. Lamont gently pushed her back and stood up, placing his plate on the windowsill beside him. "We need to prepare for this evening," he announced sternly.

Justine stretched herself out and reached up towards Lamont's waist, trying to pull him closer, but he pushed her away roughly.

"No," he said in a hollow tone. "Get dressed, we've much to do."

Justine suddenly felt uneasy, the atmosphere having developed an oppressive weight of danger. Lamont didn't look vulnerable naked. On the contrary, he seemed to radiate a strength that you could argue was almost masked by the clothes he wore as though they encumbered him.

She muttered a quiet apology and collected her clothes from the floor before pulling on her knickers and socks. She glanced up occasionally at Lamont whilst putting on her shirt and jeans, noting his vacant expression as though there was a void of darkness behind his eyes. She'd seen it before, of course. It was the look their leader wore when considering something unthinkable.

She felt herself becoming aroused again, thoughts of darkness turning her on despite his admonishment moments earlier. She knew she'd got off lightly with a stern word. There wasn't room for debate in the Branch. The puritanical rules were broken at the individual's sufferance and suffer they would if they fell short of their founder's expectations. Susan had found that out the hard way, though Justine still found it amusing the lengths Bekki had gone to in her pursuit of metering out punishment.

She found herself remembering her first meeting with their founder. Amongst the vast emptiness of the house, which was warm but at the same time bereft of anything resembling comfort, she'd first met the person who would define her future.

Flanked by a few men and women, talking and laughing quietly amongst themselves, she'd thought they had looked like an angel; strong, powerful and with a presence which filled the room with electricity. When they'd looked up unblinkingly from their position on the sofa, she'd felt as though their minds had touched.

The founder had stood up and moved towards her, placing arms around her waist and pulling her closer. She hadn't resisted as hands slid down to her hips and began to move her body. Justine had suddenly felt wanted in a way she'd never before experienced. Not sensually, but emotionally.

After her parents had died when she was sixteen, Justine had simply drifted through life, working in bars, as a stripper, in a supermarket… jobs which were empty and unrewarding. She had believed that, with no siblings to care for or reciprocate the desire, she was destined to live a lonely existence without purpose. A journey through life with no destination.

But that meeting, after being wrapped in someone's thrall, she'd felt as though their bodies had passed through each other. Call it metaphysical, spiritual or transcendental, it had felt real to her.

The founder had pulled her close and whispered in her ear. "You're doing great. That's good. Within your true self, there is no repetition. Nothing is ever the same. No moves, no actions. Everything is singular and unique. Everything is new."

As the music had faded, Justine had been held at arm's length and stared at. "You are beautiful. You need to be with me… with us. You need to be free to find your place in the world. You need to understand the part you play in what is to come."

She'd said thank you and had introduced herself. "I'm Justine Machin."

"Pleased to meet you, Justine. My name's…"

A knock at the door broke her reverie, bringing her back to

the present. Lamont was now dressed in the same clothes he always wore; white shirt, black trousers and matching brogues, polished to the point they resembled a reflective surface.

He'd certainly begun to embrace the part he'd been given, often stating that it was only stereotyping which enforced the perception that individuals such as himself should be scruffy. "If one believes himself to be superior to others, he should at least dress the part, don't you agree?" she'd heard him say before.

He drifted past Justine and opened the door just enough for her to catch sight of Angela Lockwood, one of her fellow Obadians.

"It's done," was her only response.

Lamont turned to Justine wearing a smile that betrayed all innocence. Even knowing him the way she did, she couldn't stop her body giving off an exaggerated shudder.

"How do you solve a problem like O'Connell?" he asked gleefully, the lilt in his voice almost childlike and at odds with his usual demeanour. "Dress the fox like a chicken and you won't have to force it into the hen house, it'll be welcomed."

'…fool me once, shame on me… fool me twice… I deserved to get fucked over.'

Derekica Snake

SIM WAS BANGING ABOUT THE KITCHEN, SEEMINGLY HAVING great difficulties making two cups of tea.

Joe popped his head around the doorframe. "Everything okay?"

"You can go get fucked," Sim instructed, slamming the cups down on the worktop before pouring hot water into them so mindlessly it splashed over the sides. "You know how much I hate having strangers here. No, correction, you know how much I hate people in general being in my home, in my vicinity, in the same solar system as me."

"I know," Joe replied as reassuringly as possible. "And you know I wouldn't ask if it wasn't important. Yours is the safest place in this country. You're so far off the grid, even Joe Lefores couldn't track you."

Sim stirred the tea violently and spun around to stare at Joe. "Don't quote fuckin' *Butch Cassidy and The Sundance Kid* to me. This whole situation has messed with my karma, not to mention causing my IBS to kick off. If I get piles, it's your fault."

"Fair enough," Joe agreed, moving up behind her and giving her a huge hug. "You know I love ya."

She handed Joe one of the cups and moved past him into the living room, sipping her tea slowly as she went. "Who is she anyway? This woman currently sleeping in my bed. Normally I'd be thrilled, but then again normally I'd get to choose them."

Joe sat in the swivel chair alongside her bank of computer screens and gently moved it around from side to side. Coloured lights blinked unsequentially all around him and screensavers danced across numerous monitors. The room felt as though it was possessed with an energy waiting to be tapped into. Joe turned his attention back to Sim.

"She came to me yesterday claiming to have information on whose behind all of this."

"All of this," Sim echoed mockingly.

"All right, all of that," he said, pointing at the front cover of the newspaper on her table blaring the headline **POLICE HUNT FOR MURDERER CONTINUES.**

"She says she was a member of the Obadians."

"Coincidence," Sim said knowingly.

"Don't worry," Joe assured her. "I thought that too and still do. But you know me, when would I ever let something as inconvenient as a potential set-up that might lead to my death get in the way of a good story?"

"You're a dick."

"Ah, but I'm your dick."

Sim grimaced. "Okay, moving on. You were saying…?"

Joe finished his tea and placed the cup in front of one of the computer keyboards before noticing Sim's admonishing look and moving it onto the table behind him.

"Do me a favour," Joe asked, casting a glance around the room to ensure they were alone. "Can you work your magic and dig something up on her?"

"See, you're suspicious too!"

Sim sat down at the Mac and began typing, her fingers flicked so quickly over the white keyboard that they barely appeared to touch it. Joe was a two-finger typist, but it had gotten him by in journalism. "*Do you want it quick or amazing*?" he used to say to Ciaran, his former editor at *The Daily Eire*. "*I just fucking want it*," would be his erstwhile boss's response.

He felt a momentary pang of sadness thinking about his former employer. He'd loved his job at the paper. It had given him a purpose, focus and an opportunity to make a difference amongst the journalistic elite; report the truth instead of the sensational. In the end, Obadiah Stark's story had been both, though he hadn't realised that at the time. He often blamed everything that had happened to him on his investigation into Stark but was now beginning to wonder if he'd partly brought it on himself. If he'd have left it alone like he was warned too, he would still have a career in journalism. Then again, maybe it had presented him with an opportunity. He hadn't quite decided yet.

"Well, that's impossible!" Sim's exclamation brought Joe back into the moment.

"What? What is it?"

She took a deep breath before speaking. "Okay, so I just spoke to this guy I know who used to be part of Darkode before it was shut down by the F.B.I."

"Darkode?"

"Cybercriminal forum specialising in hacking, botnets and malware amongst other illicit services."

"Oh, okay. Carry on," Joe said, despite not really understanding any of what Sim had just said.

"He can find information on pretty much anything and anyone. Everyone has a digital fingerprint, whether it be the IP address of your computer, your credit card, direct debits or your web browser. Everything leaves a sign that you were there. You know when you're searching for something on Google and then an advert pops up identifying the city you live in or things of interest to you. That's it at work at a basic level. The systems pull out keywords and use them to personalise your experience."

"Interesting... and slightly disconcerting," Joe said, scratching at the beard that now occupied his lower jaw. "What does this have to do with Maxine?"

"Nobody can live in this day and age and not leave some sign that they exist. It's impossible that someone could have never used a credit card, made an electronic transaction, held a bank account, been arrested, requested a driving licence, whatever it might be. But your fuck buddy... there's nothing."

Joe pulled his chair closer to Sim's computer screen. "She's not my fuck buddy… and there's nothing? At all?"

"Nope," she replied with an air of admiration in her voice. "Not a sausage. Effectively, she doesn't exist."

"How is that even possible?"

"Well, it's possible if someone has been able to completely remove themselves from every database in the world which is…"

"…unlikely?" Joe interrupted.

"Indeed," Sim confirmed. "I have elderly relatives who are on some of these databases – Intelius, PeopleFinders, Peekyou, Pipl – who have never been on the Internet much less ever turned on a computer. But public records, marriage and death certificates, property and so on have put them there. Now you can delete yourself from online accounts such as Facebook, Twitter, Flickr, gaming sites, close associated accounts etc. and you can weasel your way out of undeletable accounts by removing every last scrap of information about yourself. Leaving fields blank, creating new email addresses and associating undeletable accounts with this new email and then cancelling it. It's a huge arse and takes time, but it is doable, however removing yourself from the Dark Web is virtually unheard of."

"Dark Web?" Joe asked, his genuine interest illustrated by his further shuffling forward on his chair to be closer to the screen.

"It's a collection of technologies and sites that don't just hide data but conceal attempts to access it. Want a hitman hiring, or looking to purchase a nuclear warhead, link in with Islamic jihadists or have a penchant for kiddy porn? That's where you'll find it. It's actually one of the world's worst kept secrets and one of the most dangerous cyber-locations on the planet. Get a bunch of people together and give them complete anonymity and freedom from any accountability and often their worst impulses will dominate. Not the best."

"That's actually terrifying," Joe said.

"That it is," Sim agreed. "But again, she should exist somewhere, so…"

"… so?"

"So, the only other likely option is that she isn't who she says she is. She's going under an alias to hide her true identity. In that case, we'll need more than what we have. We'll need something related to her past… a name, a birthplace, even her first car. Something we can use as a frame of reference."

Joe leant back in the chair and joined his fingers together in a steeple beneath his chin. "Well, that just makes my surprise visitor all the more intriguing and suspicious."

Sim nodded in agreement. "This is too neat. You just happen to be investigating her David Koresh wannabes and she turns up with 'vital' information relating to them on your doorstep."

Joe noted the concern in her voice. "I know. But whilst she's with us, we should at least try and make her useful. I'll see what I can get from her and then let Heather know and they can take her in. Once they do that, I imagine she'll quickly become uncooperative, so we need to do it sooner rather than later. And if she is what she claims to be – a runaway from this cult – then she'll be safe with the Gardaí."

Sim shrugged, her way of agreeing with him whilst telling him he was an idiot. He stood to allow her past as she made her way to the kitchen to make them more drinks.

Sitting back down, Joe felt his sense of comfort moving away with her. Even in her modest flat, it already seemed too distant to call back.

'Men never do evil so completely and cheerfully as when they do it from religious conviction.'

Blaise Pascal

Lᴙɴsᴇʏ ᴘᴜʟʟᴇᴅ ᴜᴘ ᴛʜᴇ ᴄᴏʟʟᴀʀ ᴏF ʜᴇʀ ᴄᴏᴀᴛ ᴀɴᴅ ʟɪFᴛᴇᴅ her hands to her shoulders, rubbing them to try and stay warm.

The moon cast a web of silence over Hanover Quay, the sleek glass façade and panoramic waterfront projecting a sense of vibrancy that only added to her sense of unease. Google, Facebook, HSBC - all had offices here, its international flavour exemplifying IPUT's portfolio as a lead domestic investor in Ireland's office market and demonstrating how you can illustrate what €1.6 billion looks like. The Quay also represented everything that their leader despised about the corporate elite and 1% of those in Ireland who felt they deserved their wealth.

Lynsey checked her watch and scanned her surroundings. Justine had been gone for longer than they'd discussed. Twenty minutes had been agreed; forty minutes had passed. She was starting to worry something had gone wrong.

The sound of the Liffey flowing by in the distance was almost deafening in the silence. She strolled over to the Grand Canal Dock and looked at the moon's reflection in its waters like an oscillating mirror. Her face shimmered back at her – pale, distorted, formless. Lynsey wondered if it was now a reflection of her soul, the water showing her true self to its lone observer.

A plane leaving Dublin Airport passed overhead in the darkness, its position lights looking like solitary red, green and white stars blinking in the sky. Her gaze followed the craft and settled on the apartment buildings to her right. If Justine didn't hurry up, she would have to go and get her.

How long did it take to fucking kidnap someone?

Alison Clime was looking forward to sliding into her bed. She even contemplated not getting undressed and just climbing in as was. Work had been hell, what with the murder the other night and the world and his wife clambering for column space. Writing the entertainment and gossip column had become less about fashion and pregnancies and more about scandals and political relations. It was a far cry from the 'tits and arse' journalism that Joe O'Connell had used to call it.

She considered how the paper hadn't been the same since Joe and Ciaran had left. Joe had brought an air of enthusiasm and drive rarely seen nowadays. But after the whole Stark thing, one day he just hadn't turned up for work. He'd never told her what had happened to him or his reason for leaving, simply saying if she ever needed him he'd be there for her. She'd almost called on him a number of occasions, mostly when she was drunk and lonely, but had never found the nerve to finish dialling the number.

As for Ciaran, *The Daily Eire* had been his life and a better boss you couldn't have found. Temperamental? Definitely. Loud and angry? Often. But she'd never known a more gentle or generous soul than her former editor.

Alison understood his reason for leaving. The only thing he adored more than his job was Sue, his wife. After her diagnosis, Alison had seen the life slowly ebb from his face, day after day, as though her physical suffering from cancer was symbiotically affecting him too. His heart became less focused on his day job and more on the care he'd be providing for her that evening.

As she opened the front door and flicked on the light switch, she found herself wondering if there would ever be anyone in her life who'd feel the same about her. Someone who'd take hold of her heart and keep it safe.

It took her a few moments to realise that flicking the switch hadn't resulted in any lights. She tried it again to no avail and then internally chastised herself for doing what they always do in the movies, as though trying it more than once would miraculously make them work.

"Bollocks," Alison muttered under her breath. She took a few steps forward and froze. The huge windows at the front of her apartment allowed enough light in from the quay for her to see clearly enough. Drawers had been opened, furniture tipped over, picture frames smashed.

A nauseated feeling rose up from the bottom of her stomach, bringing with it an overwhelming urge to vomit. She felt her heart rate rising, the sound of its increasing tachycardia resonating in her ears like a pealing bell, urging her to do something to make herself feel safe in her current situation. Someone had been in her house. A stranger had entered her home and gone through her belongings.

Looking for what? Money? She didn't have any and certainly, none stashed in a mattress or behind a picture frame.

The urge to turn and run was almost irresistible, but she wanted to know what had been taken if anything.

No, get out you silly bitch!

Fishing her mobile phone from her jacket pocket with shaking fingers, Alison dialled 999 and lifted the phone to her ear whilst taking slow steps backwards towards the door she was relieved to realise she'd left open.

She was about cross the threshold when a chill coursed through her. A woman's voice came through her phone, asking for the nature of the emergency. Her voice was calming, the soft lilt of her voice making Alison consider she was probably from Cork or thereabouts. She thought it odd that in that moment of abject terror, she was momentarily considering where her potential saviour was from.

Every sinew and muscle in her body were screaming for her to move, but she was frozen to the spot, her amygdala firing out glutamate before triggering her fight or flight response by then travelling to her hypothalamus. She tried to call out but her taut vocal chords only managed a croaking squeak. There was a sharp prick in the back of her neck moments after realising someone was standing beside her. Her eyesight began to blur as her legs gave way, replaced with rubber.

As Alison fell to the floor, her body becoming soft and pliable, she heard the old television advert for Trebor Softmints reverberate in her head.

"Mr Soft, won't tell you why the world in which you're living in is so strange?"

Oh, Mr Soft, how come everything around you is so soft and rearranged."

'Seduction is always more singular and sublime than sex and it commands the higher price.'

Jean Baudrillard

THE PUB WAS CROWDED, BUT JOE WASN'T BOTHERED.

He found the claustrophobic throng of people comforting as he slowly made his way to the front of the bar and leant across the mahogany counter, signalling to Keith for his usual.

The staff in O'Dywers knew Joe well, the pub having become his home from home after Starkgate. He turned around and rested back against the bar whilst waiting for his J.D and Coke, taking stock of the bodies around him.

Spread out before him was a seemingly even selection of men and women, some laughing raucously at whatever humorous tale they were being told, others whispering softly to their partner, their heads almost touching.

He fired his most charming smile at a group of women to his left. One returned his gesture, the others just rolled their eyes at the idea of another bloke trying to get into their knickers. Judging by the size of their attire, Joe guessed it wouldn't be all that difficult.

"Here you go, mate," Keith said, placing his drink on a coaster in front of him. "€4.50."

Joe handed over the money and quickly took a large mouthful. "Rough day?" Keith asked wryly.

"Rough fucking year," Joe replied in between mouthfuls. He drained the glass of its contents and handed it back to the bartender. "Another, mate."

Keith shook his head and smiled before venturing off down the bar to collect Joe's refill.

People were jostling to get to the front of the bar whilst one man tutted loudly at Joe for blocking a prime space at the front. Joe's expression must have been more intimidating than he realised, as the man refused to make eye-contact, instead starting a conversation with his friend beside him as though he wasn't there.

Keith handed him another drink before Joe began weaving his way towards a small opening by the fire exit. He rested back against the wall and placed the glass on the table beside him.

The world around him appeared slightly surreal at that moment, his conversations with murderers and revelations about cult leaders seemingly at odds with everything else currently moving around him.

Rebecca's claim that he was somehow part of what the Branch Obadians had planned had initially seemed to Joe a mendacious statement. But what with Maxine turning up at his house and Sim's discoveries, he was starting to think

that he'd unwittingly become part of something that didn't
bode well.

How can the same shit happen to the same guy twice, Joe thought,
riffing on John McClane's famous lament.

He closed his eyes and pictured the scene that night in the
company of Obadiah Stark. He'd dreamt about it so many
times, seeing himself as though a distant observer of his
own body, restrained and in the grip of terror.

The disfigured face of Sara Jayne Morgan would stare at
him blankly, her electrolarynx making her sound more
machine than human, whilst a viewing room full of
observers looked on in glee at what was about to occur.

Murder.

With Obadiah's original execution nothing more than
smoke and mirrors, his actual death had been prepared for
that night when Joe had been captured by The Brethren
and betrayed by Vicky. All in the interests of allowing the
relatives of his victims to finally feel they'd experienced
justice through his suffering.

Obadiah's hell had been designed to see if a serial killer
could be made to feel remorse. Joe had no real idea as to
whether it had ultimately worked or not. Stark had
certainly acknowledged he'd cared for whoever he'd met
whilst in his enforced dreamscape, but whether that meant
the same as him having developed a sense of sorrow for his
crimes, Joe doubted very much.

Ultimately, it had been an exercise in proving that the
individuals who ran the country weren't the politicians or
authorities, but a cabal who appeared to have existed for

over a century in one form or another, exercising their will subversively onto its people. Joe would have laughed at the lunacy of it all if he hadn't known it to be true.

He spotted her as she effortlessly snaked between customers and tables, generating attention from the men and quite a few women, all of them looking her up and down, their attention drawn to her high-cut red dress with a large split down the side that only accentuated her long, tanned legs. Joe couldn't help but laugh at the fact that the whole seductress look was finished off with a pair of red Converse.

Maxine pushed through the crowd with ease as she made her way towards him. The world seemed to lurch into slow motion, an eternity held in a minute. Everyone took on a bullet time effect that reminded Joe of *The Matrix*. He wondered if he was already drunk, his face flushing as she stopped in front of him, biting her lip.

"Sim told me this was where you'd be," she stated knowingly. "Fuckin' glad mind. Looking like this, I'd have felt a right Muppet if you hadn't have been here."

Joe laughed. "Oh, you definitely don't look like a Muppet, or any Jim Henson character for that matter. More like Maggie Q in *Mission: Impossible*."

Maxine frowned an expression of ignorance.

"Tom Cruise? Third film? She gets out the car in a red dress with a split down the side…"

Maxine shook her head.

"Never mind," Joe said despondently. "Nice shoes by the way." He finished his drink in two mouthfuls and closed his eyes, savouring the burning sensation as it worked its way down to his stomach. When he opened them, Maxine was smiling at him. "What?"

"Nothing, you just look like you were enjoying that a little too much. Dutch courage?"

Joe laughed. "No, just anaesthetic. Anyway, what are you doing here? Is it safe for you to be out, given what you told me, which granted wasn't much."

Maxine moved to stand beside him. "Trust me, I'm safe in here. You wouldn't catch one of the Obadians in a place like this."

"A place like this?" Joe said defensively.

She put her hand on his arm in a gesture of assurance. He felt his skin tingle at her touch, even through his jacket. "I meant a pub. This kind of place is filled with the very people he feels demonstrate the very worst of humanity. Empty, needy individuals, seeking comfort in whatever and wherever they can in an effort to avoid the truth."

"Which is?"

"That the world is full of merchants and thieves whose names are interchangeable depending on who's doing the naming."

"That's… deep," Joe replied.

"Well, that's their truth, not mine. Mine is that I've had enough and have missed out on so much of life that I want to see what's waiting for me. I know there's no happy ending to any of this. Once they have you, they never let you go."

Joe felt a shiver run down his spine at her chilling words. Keen to break the uncomfortable silence, he spoke up.

"I know," he announced suddenly. "You fancy going somewhere else?"

Maxine frowned. "What's wrong with here?"

"Nothing," Joe said. "It's just seeing someone like you dressed like that in here is about as frequent an occurrence as hearing a woman say 'My, what an attractive scrotum you have.' Never happens. And besides, however safe you might feel, you're definitely drawing attention, so if I may…"

Joe put his hand on his hip for Maxine to link into. She smiled and nodded acknowledgement before placing her arm through his. As they made their way towards the exit, Joe's nerves ached as though they'd been stripped raw. His every instinct told him this was wrong. He didn't think you got to become a part of The Branch Obadians by being squeaky clean. Yet he also knew he needed information and getting her comfortable would be the best way to obtain it. He'd deal with the ramifications at a later date.

He was tired of being anxious and afraid. He wanted, just for one night, to feel as though he wasn't running head-first into a clusterfuck of immense proportions.

Again.

Lamont stood outside Kenmare Station, watching the officers through the backlit windows. They appeared so tiny, like dolls in a toy house. He guessed they *were* toys in a sense. They were being played with, manipulated and being moved around the chessboard. Their lack of insight into what they'd become involved in almost made him laugh out loud.

The muted sky seemed to be aware of what was about to occur, grey clouds sombre and almost oppressive. He heard thunder crack in the distance, nature's way of reminding the human race of just who was in charge.

As the rain beat down, hammering the pavement, vehicles and people around him, Lamont took a deep breath. What had been set in motion had been important. What he was about to do now was necessary.

The view into the Gardaí station was now blurred by rain streaming down the glass. It mattered little to Lamont.

They would all see clearly soon enough.

This is a huge fucking mistake, Joe thought as he peeled off Maxine's dress.

They'd left O'Dywers and had ended up in Turner's Lounge for the remainder of the evening. Joe had resisted becoming too journalistic, instead finding himself just enjoying her company. She had a freedom in the way she spoke that he found refreshing. He wasn't certain whether her outlook on life had been influenced by the Branch or the other way around; always there but inhibited and the Branch had helped free that part of her. Yet, the entire time he knew he was digging himself into a hole so huge Indiana Jones wouldn't be able to find him.

He hadn't informed Heather about her, instead sequestering Maxine away at Sim's whilst he tried to work out the most productive way in which to use her and the information she may well hold. He didn't want to interfere with the investigation, merely to know why these Obadians seemed so interested in him. He knew it had to do with Stark, but he just couldn't work out how.

She kissed him passionately as her dress slipped to the floor, stepping out of it whilst at the same time pushing Joe back against the bed and falling on top of him. Joe was a little surprised by Maxine's forcefulness, her lack of consideration for the niceties of seduction instead replaced by animalistic passion.

As she pulled his shirt off and his trousers down, Joe felt her pull her knickers aside and roughly force him inside of her. What had begun as a potentially romantic moment had taken on a cruder meaning, with an air of aggression and bleakness that could be equated to assault.

He felt her bite his neck and his chest, her body writhing slowly but urgently against his. Joe realised he was a passive participant in his own sexual encounter, something pleasurable yet, at the same time oddly uncomfortable. If he'd still been working at the paper, he'd either be facing the sack or a severe fucking, less enjoyable than the one he was experiencing. He knew well all the horror stories a la Suzy Wetlaufer who'd become romantically involved with her source from General Electric in America and had lost her job once it had become public knowledge.

But he wasn't a reporter anymore, so the only problem he had was that of non-disclosure of a potential witness to an on-going investigation that could see him arrested.

Joe felt Maxine's body tense and begin to shudder just

moments before he climaxed. She collapsed on top of him, their heavy breathing the only sound filling his bedroom.

Lifting her head she smiled at Joe, sweat matting hair to her forehead. "I like your interpretation of keeping me safe, Mr O'Connell."

"Well, not exactly what I had in mind and something I'll most likely regret."

Maxine climbed off Joe and sat back. "Fuck you very much. What a charmer you are."

He tried to reach for her as she slid towards the edge of the bed and stood up. "Sorry, that came out wrong," he said contritely. "I meant that not only did we only just meet, but I've just slept with a witness in a huge murder investigation. I'm the fucking idiot. I know better."

"You hardly forced yourself on me, Joe," Maxine said reassuringly, sitting back down beside him. "I've been ostracised from the world for so long. Granted, initially by my own choice, but now I'm out here there are so many things I've missed out on, random sex with a virtual stranger one of them."

Joe couldn't help but smile at her comment, gently caressing the back of her neck.

"That feels good," she sighed.

"That's twice you've said that to me. I'm honoured," he joked.

She chuckled as his hands moved down her back and up again.He paused just below her shoulder blades, suddenly having a flashback to the photograph he'd seen of Rebecca when looking through her file. A feeling he couldn't place descended on him. Curiosity mixed with something else. Suspicion perhaps. "Rebecca…"

Maxine turned to face him. "Thinking of another woman already, are we?"

Joe shook his head. "No, well, yes but not like that. When she was arrested, I noticed there was something buried under the skin around her shoulder. Like an implant. She wouldn't tell me what it was – You don't have one."

Maxine fell silent. Joe moved around the bed and took her hand. "What is it? You came to me remember, but I can't help you if you don't help me."

"I know," she replied quietly. "It's not something I want to talk about right now."

"Nevertheless, you said you'd tell me everything."

"And you'll get to know everything, I promise," she replied, leaning over to kiss him on the forehead. "Let me grab a shower and a cup of coffee, and then we can talk. I'll tell you whatever you want to hear. Fair enough?"

Joe grabbed Maxine's hand as she rose from the bed. "No, tell me something now. I think I've earned it and I don't mean just the sex. This whole thing is insane. I need to know I can trust you."

Her eyes darted across every part of Joe's face, as though looking for a flaw or contradiction in his plea. Finding nothing, Maxine nodded once and sat back down on the bed, angled slightly away from Joe. Her eyes took on a distant look as she began to speak.

"I came to you because you're the only person I know who can help me. I read about you, your work on The Tally

Man and all the other cases you've reported on. You're a respected reporter…"

"Was," Joe interjected.

"…was," Maxine repeated. "But you still have all those instincts that made you good at your job. Now, I don't know much but I can tell you something I heard… a word. I don't know what it means."

"What was the word," Joe asked, his skin prickly with anticipation and foreboding as though his subconscious knew what she was about to say.

Maxine turned and looked at him, her eyes unblinking. "Brethren."

She hesitated for a moment before heading off in the direction of the bathroom.

Joe was frozen to the spot, almost having to force himself to lie back on the bed.

Fuck, fuck, fuck, fuck!

He'd known there'd been something from the start, the moment Rebecca Sill had asked for him. Obadiah Stark was stuck to him like a shadow, even in death haunting his every move. Not only could he not sleep because of the man, but it seemed that no matter what he did he was never going to escape his presence.

But there was something else that bothered him more than that. A feeling. Something ominous - as though he'd opened Pandora's Box and it was too late to close it. The final lock had been broken, the dangers inside provided a means of escape. Clive Barker's *Lemarchand's Configuration Box* made real in the form of a cult, its occupants not deformed scarified priests but men and women whose desires for inflicting pain represented their own form of pleasure.

Joe wondered if this was how Michael Douglas's character had felt when asking for the cheque in *Fatal Attraction*.

That he'd just made a mistake. A terrible mistake.

'Insight into character comes from listening intently to the spoken word. The physical person, their charisma, charm and dramatic flair is more often used to persuade audiences, as they use these stealth tools of disguise and deception.'

Maximillian Degenerez

Lamont stood inside the entrance to the Gardaí station, amused at the hive of activity buzzing before him.

He realised they were just like ants, scurrying around aimlessly to the point of appearing directionless. And how do you get rid of ants? You stamp on them.

Lamont unbuttoned his black jacket and wafted off the rain that had soaked it whilst stood outside. No one paid any attention to him, but then again why would they? For all intents and purposes, he was just a man here to either report a crime or ask for advice.

"Good evening, officer," Lamont announced as he approached the counter. "I was wondering if I could speak to Joe O'Connell. I understand he's assisting you with the murder of Susan Bradley."

The booking sergeant managed to look confused and surprised at the same time. "May I ask the nature of your request," he replied warily.

"Of course you can," Lamont answered politely. "I'm the individual who orchestrated the murder of said Susan Bradley."

The desk sergeant paused for a moment, letting what he'd just heard sink in. He gestured to two officers behind him and whispered something as they flanked him.

Lamont looked amused as they walked out from behind the counter and positioned themselves at either side. "You'll have to wait here a moment," the sergeant instructed, the anxiety in his voice apparent.

"Certainly," Lamont replied cordially.

Whereupon his entrance, the bodies in the station had been moving frenetically and talking incessantly, now a hush fell over the entire building. It was as though the news of his statement had already circulated to everyone present as fast as blood circulates the body. Some were pointing and whispering in muted conversation, others looked angry, some just surprised.

Lamont thought it comical how you could alter the entire sense of purpose in a room with just a few words. They understood so little and he found himself wondering when was the last time they'd felt anything with any passion?

He knew what it was like to be truly free to explore your will and darkest desires. The most freedom they'd probably ever experienced was deciding which Pot Noodle to have.

A stern-looking woman appeared from an office towards the back of the station, striding purposefully towards him as though not reaching him in time would hold a consequence.

"I'm Detective Inspector Heather Robinson. I understand

you have information relating to a current murder investigation."

Lamont laughed, the sound fat with contempt. "I do indeed. It was I who has been the architect of all that has occurred. In the meantime, I'd like to speak to Joe O'Connell."

Heather tried to contain her anger, whispering under her breath. "Oh, for fuck's sake."

"I'll only speak to Joe O'Connell."

"What is it with everyone we arrest at the moment only wanting to speak to that reporter? Does he have you on retainer?"

"Amusing," Lamont replied. "However, in regards to answers, I'll only speak to Joe O'Connell."

If Heather's expression could have been made tangible, the whole building would have spontaneously combusted from the fury in her eyes. She gestured behind her with a thumb. "Get him booked in and put him in holding."

Lamont nodded politely towards her as the officers flanking him took his arms and escorted him to the rear of the building.

She turned to the sergeant, trying to relax her twisted features. "Find O'Connell and tell him to get here, right now. If he gives you any excuses, arrest him."

The sergeant nodded and hurried away. Heather returned to her office and slammed the door with more force than intended. The man who'd just presented himself should have been a victory if what he'd said turned out to be true, yet it didn't feel particularly satisfying for two reasons. One was she was suspicious of his motives. No one just hands themselves in and claims to have been responsible for murder unless they have an agenda. Which led to her second concern – Joe O'Connell.

As irritating as it was that he seemed to be the focal point of a huge murder investigation, she had an uneasy feeling she couldn't shake regarding his involvement. Not that Heather believed he was guilty of anything. On the contrary, he had already been a huge help, though she'd never have told him. But the fact that two suspects in a crime had both demanded to speak to him meant there was more going on than simple altruistic behaviour from potential murderers keen to provide the details needed to solve a case.

Something…Something…Something…

Heather made her way out of the office and towards The Box to review the man who'd just turned himself in. As she walked, the curiousness of the whole situation continued to unsettle her, the answer teasing her beyond the limits of her reach.

Hauntingly familiar. Terrifyingly nameless.

'The basic tool for the manipulation of reality is the manipulation of words. If you can control the meaning of words, you can control the people who must use the words.'

Phillip K. Dick

FEBRUARY 26TH 21:17

KENMARE (AN NEIDIN) COUNTY KERRY, IRELAND

"Sɪᴛ ᴅᴏᴡɴ," Hᴇᴀᴛʜᴇʀ ɪɴsᴛʀᴜᴄᴛᴇᴅ Jᴏᴇ ᴡʜᴏ ᴅᴜʟʏ ᴅɪᴅ sᴏ on the chair behind him.

He'd been concerned when the two officers had knocked at his door half an hour ago, thinking that somehow someone had learnt of Maxine. They hadn't told him why he had to accompany them, only that he did with a sense of urgency.

Heather picked up an elastic band and began rotating it around her index fingers. Her gaze was intense, making Joe feel as though she was trying to see inside his soul.

"If this is about me getting banned from that slow-cooker class on Facebook?"

"What?"

"I joined a slow-cooker group but was banned because I'd already joined another one and they didn't like it."

"Don't be a smart arse, you'll only embarrass yourself," Heather responded.

"Even more than being banned from a slow-cooker group? I doubt that."

Joe could tell from her expression that Heather wasn't in the mood for him being glib.

"I don't know if I can trust you, Joe."

"Wow, as openers go, that's reassuring."

"Well, I'm sorry but that happens to be the truth. You were a premier reporter, a brilliant investigator as I'm led to believe and allegedly universally lauded for your work on the Stark case, if case is the right word, for the whole conspiracy theories surrounding that bastard."

"Listen…"Joe began to interject. Heather waved his interruption away.

"I'm not interested in any of that. What I am interested in is that we now have a man in custody claiming to have been involved in, or in his words, orchestrated, the murder of Susan Bradley and who wants to specifically speak to you."

"Oh," Joe said.

"Oh, indeed," Heather snapped. "That's two murder suspects who'll only talk to you. Not only is it highly irregular, frankly it's got me fucking concerned. What's going on, Joe? No bullshit."

He stood up and began pacing around the office, fishing around in his pockets for his cigarettes. He pulled one out and went to light it.

"Uh uh," Heather intoned. "Not in here."

"What are you gonna do? Arrest me?"Joe said in a snarky voice.

"I could arrest you at the moment on a number of things, so yes I will if you light that thing."

Joe looked to see if she was bluffing but decided she looked all too genuine and reluctantly placed the cigarette in the packet before sitting back down. He took a deep breath and considered carefully what he was about to say. "I have no idea what any of this has to do with me, that's the truth. I'd never met Rebecca Sill before nor do I know why they seemed so interested in me, but…"

"Well?" Heather asked after a few moments silence.

Joe shuffled uncomfortably. "A woman turned up at my house the other night, claiming to be from the cult who's behind all of this."

Heather's expression was one of disbelief. Joe carried on before she had a chance to respond.

"She came to me claiming I was the only one who could help her. Told me she'd run away from them, that she didn't believe in what they stood for anymore."

Heather flicked the elastic band towards the bin in the corner. "Go on," she said impatiently.

"So, a lady calling herself Maxine comes to my house asking me to protect her in exchange for telling me all she knows about the Branch Obadians, the cult that Rebecca is a member of and who, I'm assuming, the man you have in custody is also."

"Christ Almighty," Heather exclaimed. "A fucking has-been reporter knows more about this investigation than the actual police!" Joe bent forward over Heather's desk.

"Look, be angry with me later. Arrest me, whatever. The fact is that we… you, have a bigger problem than me knowing more. There's something going on, a bigger picture and we're missing it. Maxine told me these people are obsessed with Obadiah Stark, I mean his whole twisted philosophy on the world and how we were just cattle, ambling about waiting to be picked off by the strongest predators. The whole thing's just off. I mean, think about it. Rebecca Sill has an implant in her back. Have you removed it yet to find out what it is?"

Heather look momentarily embarrassed. "No," she mumbled. "There's some sort of Human Rights bollocks we have to circumvent before we can 'operate' on her." She mimicked quotation marks in the air as she spoke.

"Well, you need to do it and fast. The fact they all seem to want to speak to me means it has something to do with Obadiah, I just can't figure out what. Though this afternoon I came a step closer to maybe taking an educated guess."

"And…?" Heather insisted.

"You remember Rebecca mentioning The Brethren during her interview?"

Heather nodded.

"Well, their name came up again today, but in the worst possible way."

"Meaning?" Heather was growing both impatient and curious.

"Meaning," Joe said resignedly. "That I think they're involved somehow. I don't know in what respect exactly, but Maxine told me she'd heard their name mentioned. And despite their projected image of altruism, I don't think he's looking to hire them for quashing a parking ticket."

Heather's body looked like it was suddenly melting from beneath her, forcing her to slump forward on the desk and rest her head in her hands. When she spoke again, her voice sounded weak. Joe was used to her self-assertiveness and assurance. She suddenly sounded like an old woman – vulnerable and frail.

"You know, I joined the force because I wanted to be part of something bigger than I was. I know most people will say they joined to make a difference or to help people, but I just wanted to know that despite being only a small cog in a large wheel, one act, however big or small, could make the biggest difference in someone's life. And of course, you dream of THE big case, the one that'll define your career for the rest of your life. I was jealous of you, you know."

Joe's eyes softened, encouraging her to go on. Not for his own ego, but to keep her talking. He knew it was a moment of honesty they were sharing that meant something.

"Your coverage of the Stark case had us all hooked. You had a knack for not sensationalising his crimes, yet at the same time drawing attention to the fact he was a monster. Christ, you even made him sound almost sympathetic sometimes, which is quite a feat for a serial killer. We were all waiting for your book on him. We actually believed we'd learn something from you about how the mind of a psychopath worked, did you know that?"

Joe shook his head gently.

"You were quite the celebrity in the law enforcement world. And then, you just fell off the face of the earth. No book ever materialised, you left the paper… what happened?"

Joe considered his next words carefully, having never uttered them to another living soul since the night of Stark's real execution. Even Sim didn't know the details. "The Brethren happened," he said, feeling oddly relieved at saying it out loud.

"Stark's execution was just for show, a misdirection to appease the public and the press. He was actually executed a few weeks later in my presence in a facility occupied by the relatives of his victims, government officials and members of The Brethren who'd planned the whole thing."

He could see the disbelief forming on Heather's face.

"Their public persona, the one that claims they'll get justice for you? It's a front. Yeah, they do actually do some of that for real, though how genuinely heartfelt it actually is I have no idea. But their real work is in bringing justice by any means necessary to those people who feel the system has let them down, as in 'execution for a serial killer isn't punishment enough' kind of way.

"Stark was sedated the night of his state execution, moved to an undisclosed location, placed in some sort of stasis where he was injected with psychotropic drugs that made him think he was living another life where he had a family, the purpose being that if he was made to care about something and then had it taken away from him, albeit fictionally, then he might in some way understand the loss the relatives of his victims had felt. Then, in front

of a specially selected audience, he was executed
for real."

"And you were there?" Heather asked in disbelief. "You
saw these people? Saw him killed?"

"Yup," came Joe's nonchalant response. "The only person
who's seen a serial killer executed twice. Who knew?"

Heather was watching Joe steadily, a faint smile on her lips.
"You know, I actually believe you."

"I damn well hope so, 'cause I was warned that night if I
ever mentioned anything about what or who I'd seen then
I'd find myself with an umbrella up my arse being opened,
metaphorically speaking. Hence no book, no job and no
fucking life. My obsession with Obadiah Stark and finding
out the truth about his 'execution' led me down a road that
certainly wasn't paved with yellow bricks. More like a
whole load of fucks and bollocks."

"Metaphorically speaking," Heather repeated with a smile
that Joe found himself instinctively returning.

"Why, Detective Inspector, did we just share a moment?"
Heather's face hardened as quickly as it had softened. "No,
you're still a dick."

"Right," Joe acknowledged without challenge. "But, I'm the
dick you appear to need right now."

"Christ, what I'm about to do is so far off the
reservation…" She inhaled deeply before speaking again.
"Same deal as before. I'm in the room, but you can have a
little more latitude in speaking to the suspect. Screw this up
and it's my job - hell, it'll probably be my job regardless.
But I need to know what's going on and I want to know
why they all have a hard-on for you."

"Trust me," Joe said, his voice laced with concern. "So do I."

"But first, there's someone I want you to meet." Heather stood and opened the door to allow Joe passage.

"Okay," he said as he rose from the chair. He felt his legs wobble slightly causing him to grab hold of its arms to steady himself. Heather moved to assist him, but he waved her away. "I'm fine," he assured her. "Just got up too fast."

They made their way to one of the offices further down the hallway where an elderly gentleman was sitting beside a desk. His tweed jacket, black trousers with a seam running down the front, tanned briefcase and small, Harry Potteresque glasses gave away the fact he was some sort of academic.

"Joe, this is Professor Richard Bellamy who specialises in Religious Studies and Sociology. After our last conversation, I reached out to a friend who directed me to him. He's seen all the information we have regarding the Obadians that I could give without specifics and said he might be able to give us some insight that may assist in the investigation. Professor Bellamy, Joe O'Connell."

He stood and shook Joe's hand firmly. "Pleasure," he said in a clipped English tone before sitting back down. "Fan of your work, very… dramatic."

"Thank you," Joe said, relaxing into one of the other vacant chairs. Heather took up a position leaning against the desk.

"Violence and religion have long been the subject of growing interest to social scientists and us scholars," the professor began. "With religion being so diverse, it stands to reason that the violence associated with some of them would be also. In the case of the Branch Obadians, or 'new religious movement' as they're termed, they not only offer radical resistance to the rigid social order but sacralise that resistance. Quite how such religious movements become involved in violent acts is something we've been studying to understand for some time, as such activities pose a theoretical and public perspective."

"So, groups such as the Mason Family, Davidians, Heaven's Gate collective…?"

"Indeed," replied the professor with an air of surprise and admiration at Joe's knowledge. "In the case of the Obadians, they found a kinship in the words of Obadiah Stark which would have instigated their 'awakening' period where their ideology is formed in order to separate them from society. People believe cults always recruit hundreds of followers, when in reality the most successful ones, in the crudest sense of the word, are the ones that have a small number of devoted followers. More people means difficulty monitoring their attitudes and behaviours; that is where dissent can breed.

This small core group then go through what is termed a'chrysalis' phase where they abandon old identities and create new ones compatible with their new-found ideology. This tightly organised group now begin to take their previous emotions concerning uncertainty and turn them into conspiracy and a belief that they are being victimised. Whilst searching for what are termed 'new options', they often, but not always, come up with an alternative line of action that will facilitate their means of reaching the next level. In the case of the Obadians, using people as their mechanism for the transition to a higher plane of existence. Usually cults such as this one claim to be doing God's work. The Obadians are unique in the fact that they make no secret that all they want is to fulfil their own needs and desires, as did Obadiah Stark. Be it through death and suffering, it doesn't really matter. They see the transcendence of their soul inexorably linked to the destruction of another's. Don't think of them as people, more monsters masquerading as such."

Heather look slightly unnerved at what she'd just heard, Joe simply fascinated. He wondered what Stark would have thought about all this – people using his name as a form of reverence. For some reason, he didn't think he would've have been that impressed, that it sullied his purpose somewhat.

"Thank you for your time, Professor," Heather said, breaking what had rapidly become an uncomfortable silence. He shook her hand and offered it to Joe, pumping it vigorously. "You're most welcome. I only hope it helps somewhat in these awful circumstances."

As they left the office and escorted Professor Bellamy out before making their way towards the Box, Joe realised he was afraid, his mind clouded with doubt as to how well this would turn out.

After what he'd just heard, perhaps the horrors he'd experienced with Obadiah Stark had only been the beginning.

'What enables us to achieve our greatness contains the seeds of our destruction.'

Jim Valvano

LAMONT SAT ACROSS THE TABLE FROM JOE AND HEATHER, his handcuffed hands resting on the surface.

His faint smile unsettled Joe. It was as though he were happy to be there – had *intended* to be there. His green eyes focused on Joe unwaveringly, challenging him to speak first.

It was Heather who broke the silence by clicking on the recorder. She turned and nodded at Joe as though indicating everything was going to be okay. But the unsettling feeling he had was getting more intense, telling him that their trouble was just about to begin. "The time is 22: 03, the date February 26th, Interview Room five. Detective Inspector Heather Robinson present with civilian Joe O'Connell. The suspect has declined legal representation." Lamont's body language spoke of someone eager to begin. "Can you state your full name for the record?" Heather asked, sounding more like a demand than a request.

"Lamont Etchison," came the polite reply. "May I ask, do

you ever wonder why madness is represented by visible, tangible interpretations?"

"What?" Heather snapped at his random question.

"Madness. *One Flew Over the Cuckoo's Nest*, *Identity* and so on. It's always stereotypical – babbling incoherently, foaming at the mouth, conspiracy theories, sharing packets of Juicy Fruit with Native Americans – it has to have a visible presence otherwise how can you make people understand what madness truly is. Clever, stupid, genius or violent, it has to have a visual manifestation or you could never truly appreciate what it's like to be mad. Not that you can from those examples. They're just bigoted generalisations from ignorant people who don't comprehend the world they live in or those who occupy it. Do you think I'm mad?"

Heather considered the question. "I can't make such an assessment. That's for the psychologist to decide. Besides, I don't even know what you're guilty of, only what you claim to have done."

"Oh, I've done what I've claimed to have done," Lamont stated proudly. "I was tasked to find willing members, lost souls with no direction and provide them with a purpose. Persuading some of them to kill for us wasn't difficult. On the contrary, it's amazing how many people have such a fantasy – to be an instrument of death. To wield that kind of power over another… Stark was right, there's no feeling like it, or so I'm told. I haven't killed anyone. Why have a dog and bark yourself."

His glibness about his actions took Joe a little by surprise. Not that he hadn't heard a sociopath's rhetoric before. They're always filled with hubris, desperate to brag about their crimes so that it'll become a matter of record that'll prolong the longevity of their persona. But Lamont didn't sound like he was boasting. He sounded like he was trying to be clever and allude to something else. Every minute sitting in the Box with him made Joe's sense of unease escalate.

"How have you managed to remain undetected for so long?" Heather asked.

Lamont shrugged. "Patience, planning and puritanism - the good old three P's. Obadiah Stark deserved nothing less than a fully committed, devoted representation of his beliefs. Finding those kinds of people takes time, so once you have them you're required to utilise them carefully, otherwise it's all been for nothing."

Just as Heather was about to respond, Lamont bounced up from his chair and flicked his finger off the tip of her nose, as fast as a frog's tongue. He sat back down and leant forward, dropping his voice to a whisper and placing his cuffed hands on her arm. Heather found herself simultaneously surprised and disgusted; the latter because she thought he was odious, but the former because it felt nice.

He slid them up and down the crook of her arm, staring at her intently. "See, this is how it is. You can't say no. There is no saying no. You go with the flow."

Heather found herself nodding because, at that moment, she could understand how it was. His hands on her skin felt good, unexpectedly so.

Joe just glared incredulously at what was unfolding before him. It was as though Lamont was a presence, demonstrating how easy it was for him to have people do the things he wanted them to do. Joe knew he was no

Svengali, but he certainly thought he might be a Charles Manson.

"There isn't anyone I can't touch on the nose," Lamont proclaimed, tilting his head to one side. "I know what you're thinking. If I can touch you, I can kill you. Don't worry, this isn't about you."

He moved his hands away and placed them back beneath the table.

"So, what *is* it about then?" Heather asked, the tremor noticeable in her voice. She shuddered, as though the very thought of having enjoyed his touch had repulsed her.

He turned his head slowly and stared at Joe. "It's about him."

"Why me?"

"Because we have something of yours that you'll want back and will only get back if you tell me all you know about The Brethren's involvement in the murder of Obadiah Stark."

"I have no idea what you're talking about," Joe replied with as much poise as he could muster. He racked his brain, trying to think of something they could have of his that would mean enough to him to use as leverage, but he came up empty. He had no family, no partner and no money. "Besides, I have nothing worth taking and you're full of shit. Why go to all this trouble, get yourself arrested when you could have just contacted me anyway? Rebecca made it clear you knew all about me, so you could have just turned up my house, done whatever you needed to, got what you want and then left and no one would have been any the wiser. Why this elaborate and frankly, stupid plan to get yourself arrested?"

"Oh, Joe you are so wrong. You have everything worth taking. You've never faced your pain, always running away from it. Yeah, you've stayed ahead of it for a while, but now it's caught up with you it'll be unforgiving."

Joe wondered if his swallow had been audible. Heather was beginning to shift uncomfortably in her seat, as though she was ready to end the interview.

"And," he said in a low tone, leaning forward ever so slightly. "It isn't a stupid plan, trust me." He sat back and reassumed his relaxed position. "So, why don't you just stop being coy and tell me about The Brethren." His tone was damningly precise because of his complete lack of inflexion when he spoke.

"I told you, I don't know what you're talking about."

"You don't? You weren't at a facility the night he was murdered by a collective group of corrupt government officials and bleeding heart relatives. Or in other words, a pack of cunts."

Joe glanced at Heather beside him, uncertain of how to respond. He didn't even have the first clue how Lamont could know any of that. The only other person he had told was Heather earlier.

"Look," Lamont said with an impatient sigh. "Tell me or Alison Climi joins our growing list of Tally Man homages."

The look on Joe's face must have been extreme as it promoted Lamont to utter a laugh on the wrong side of dirty.

"Your former workplace flirt bot? A few of the Branch are probably getting to know her quite well by now."

Flying out of his seat, Joe grabbed Lamont by the collar of his shirt. Heather signalled to the one-way viewing window for help and tried to loosen his grip on her suspect. Two officers burst into the room seconds later and flanked him on either side, pulling him back towards his chair with enough force he automatically let go of Lamont, but not before pulling him across the table slightly.

Lamont attempted to straighten his shirt as much as he could with his hands cuffed and shook his head while tutting at Joe disappointedly.

"Now, do you really think that kind of behaviour is going to accomplish anything?" His tone was reminiscent of a school teacher admonishing his class. Lamont briefly scanned the walls of the room. "By the way, does anyone have the time?"

"Why?" Heather asked.

"Oh, come on. Knowing the time isn't infringing on any potential investigation, is it?"

Heather glanced at her watch. "Twenty-five to ten."

"Thank you," he replied almost gleefully. Joe felt as though he would have clapped his hands together had they been free.

Joe tried to shrug off the hands of the officers pinning him to his chair. He looked at Heather appealingly, prompting her to nod for them to release him. She gave him another look that simply said *behave*.

"All right, let's cut the crap," Joe demanded, banging on

the table with his fist. Heather shook her head but didn't intervene. "Where's Alison? Why take her? She only worked with me. Christ, our desks weren't even that close together."

Lamont gestured for Joe to move closer. "Why do you think we took her, Joe?"

"Because you need leverage," he replied after a moment's pause. "I don't tell you what you want to know and she dies."

"Bingo," Lamont shouted. "What time is it now?"

"Five minutes later than when you asked before," Heather snapped.

"Twenty to ten," Lamont confirmed to himself.

"All right, enough games. Let's go, Joe. He's just playing with us. We'll get nothing useful from him."

Heather rose from the table, leaving her chair in the middle of the floor. She was at the door when Joe called out. "Wait."

Heather looked over her shoulder; Lamont smiled knowingly. She shook her head, eyes pleading not to share with him what he'd confided in her. She knew the man before them needed to know for a reason and whatever the reason was, it wouldn't be for anything good.

"I was betrayed by someone I was seeing," Joe began, his tone representing his heavy heart at what he was about to remember. "She drugged me and when I woke, I was in some sort of facility. I don't know where only that it can't have been far and must have been in Ireland. Obadiah Stark was brought in and placed beside me in a chair – we were both restrained – and someone claiming to be the sister of the woman I'd been seeing and one of Obadiah's victims, the only one who'd survived as far as we know, explained that she worked for a company called The Brethren and that alongside their public services they also offered relatives the sort of restorative justice that you wouldn't find in the justice system."

"Go on,' Lamont ordered with a smirk.

Joe looked at him with obsidian eyes, full of hatred. "They made Stark explain what he had experienced. As far as I understood it, they'd faked his execution and placed him in some sort of stasis where he was drugged, so his subconscious made him form memories about things – people – he cared about. Then in this dreamscape, they were taken away from him so he could potentially experience loss and what it felt like. I have no idea whether it worked. He said something about having had a wife and child he almost loved but was unrepentant about being a murderer. Then they pulled back a curtain to show a viewing room full of his victim's relatives, the prison warden and others and then…"

"Then?" Lamont pushed.

"Then they executed him… for real." Joe heard it in his own voice, but couldn't quite believe it. He realised he sounded sorry for Stark.

"See, that wasn't so hard, was it? You did really well, Joe. Truly." Lamont's voice was dripping with condescending bile. "Last question – where did they take his body?"

Joe shook his head vigorously. "I have no idea. I was warned not to say anything about what I'd seen, not to write my book or else they'd kill me and I was drugged again. Next thing I knew I woke up in bed."

Lamont frowned. "That's not good enough."

"What do you want me to say?" Joe said, his voice rising slightly in frustration. "I was unconscious, ergo, i.e., therefore, I didn't see what they did with him."

Lamont seemed amused by the petulant response. "Okay, I believe you. But in that case, given what you've just told me, you'll know someone who does, yes?"

Joe realised it wasn't a question. "What do you mean?"

"Now, now, Joe. Don't spoil our friendly *tête-a-tête* when we're doing so well. You said there were others there, yes? One of them was your ex-girlfriend?"

"She wasn't my girlfriend," Joe snapped.

"Whatever" Lamont said dismissively. "However you wish to label her, she and others were there and you must know who some of them are."

Joe could feel his neck becoming crimson. He felt as though his face was on fire as it had been in the days when his Mum had caught him out doing something he shouldn't be doing.

"So, we have an understanding," Lamont announced, taking Joe's physiological response as confirmation. "And when you see him, tell him I have Subject One's journal."

Joe looked puzzled and turned to look at Heather. Her face was pale and drawn, her eyes darting between Joe and Lamont.

"Him?"

"We both know who you'll see, don't we Joe? The man so close to being a bow and arrow."

Joe was about to speak when Lamont asked for the third time. "What time is it?"

"Jesus Christ," he exclaimed in annoyance. "Ten fifty-eight."

"Well, in that case, I'd better be quick. There's a reckoning coming. What we're doing is only a small part of a larger process. Stark started it many years ago, we're continuing it in his name and then after us, there'll be others. It's never ending, a snake eating its own tale. All who have died already and those yet to, that's not the will of God, that's the will of the people. They want you all to know they've had enough. Without killing we have no chance, so you need to ask yourself how can that work for me?"

Lamont gave Joe and Heather a huge smile; a smile Joe realised represented the face of death. In hindsight what he said next should have promoted Joe to act sooner, but he hadn't realised the significance of it.

"It's okay, Joe. You don't play cards without stacking the deck first, now do you? And it won't hurt her. I imagine she won't feel a thing. They don't all have one of course. Rebecca volunteered"

At that moment, the whole building shook as though God's wraith were raining down upon them.

'Reason, I sacrifice you to the evening breeze.'

Aimé Césaire

"So, what's the plan with her?" Lynsey asked, nodding in the direction of Alison, who was tied to a bed in front of them.

Justine shrugged. "I know as much as you. Lamont said to just keep her here." She frowned slightly, the furrows on her brow visible even in the muted light of the bedroom.

"What?" Lynsey asked.

"She's hot, don't you think?"

"I'm certain he also said something about not harming her," Lynsey chastised.

"It wasn't harming her I was thinking about," Justine replied salaciously.

Lynsey grabbed her arm and spun her around "Don't touch me, you fuckin' dyke!"

Lynsey glared at her indifferently, releasing her grip. "That's rich coming from you. For a lesbian, you've seen more cock than a GUM clinic. Or are we muff-diving this week?"

Justine stepped towards the bed where Alison lay. She was moaning slightly, the Midazolam she'd been injected with appearing to wear off. It didn't provide full unconsciousness, but just enough to ensure that Alison would be unlikely to remember anything specific.

Justine had taken it once with Lamont prior to them having sex. She couldn't remember details, just a deep-seated feeling of having been somewhere pleasurable. She'd never asked him what he'd done to her whilst she'd been like that, but the subsequent ache in her arse for a few days afterwards had given her an idea. She felt herself becoming aroused just thinking about it. If chastity knickers hadn't been standing behind her, she might have indulged herself a little at Alison's expense.

Maybe later.

Sitting on the edge of the bed, Justine gently caressed Alison's face. Her moans became louder as her alert state increased, her eyes suddenly springing open. Her breathing immediately increased as her memory flooded back, the alien surroundings only compounding her agitation.

"Where… am I?"

Justine continued stroking her face. "Shhh, it's okay. You're safe. No one is going to hurt you."

Alison tried to sit up but found she couldn't. She tilted her head up towards and began thrashing angrily at the handcuffs securing her to the bed. The second set around her ankles had a shackling chain tethering them together.

Despite her efforts, her somnolent state meant her resistance was muted.

"Safe? Where the fuck am I?"

Her eyes darted frantically around the room. In the dim lighting, she could just make out a chest of drawers to her left, peeling wallpaper that was either off white or her eyes were still adjusting and a light above her with no shade. Oddly, the fact there were no windows had her more scared than anything else.

"You're our guest, temporarily," Justine replied softly, her hand moving down over Alison's neck and towards her chest. "If your ex does as he's told, then you'll be home in no time."

Alison fidgeted beneath Justine's caress, her expression a mixture of disgust and terror.

"Get your fucking hands off me! What do you mean, my ex?"

"Joe O'Connell," Justine replied, ignoring the plea to stop. "If he's shares everything we need to know, then you'll be okay. If not…"

"What do you mean, if not?" Alison cried out frantically. "What do you want with me? I haven't seen Joe since he left the paper. We worked together a few years ago... and he's not my ex. He's not my type."

"No, but you're mine," Justine said excitedly, the movement of her hands becoming more animated down Alison's gaoled body.

Neither of them noticed Lynsey move behind Justine and grab one of her hands. "That's enough. Leave her alone."

"I'd let go if I were you, bitch," came the measured response. "Otherwise you'll be struggling to wipe your arse after I break your hand."

Lynsey pulled her up roughly and span Justine round to face her. Her eyes burned with hatred in the face of the woman who was always getting in the way. Justine knew Lamont favoured her more than the rest, despite the fact she'd never given in to his advances to sleep with him. But that wasn't Justine's biggest irritation. It was the fact that he never even chastised her for it. She'd refused to sleep with him in the early days and he'd kicked the shit out of her, leaving her with a broken nose and two fractured ribs.

After that, she hadn't dared refuse again. The next time had been angry, violent and the best sex she'd ever had with either gender. One could quibble that finding someone on top and inside you when you awoke in the middle of the night was rape, but that illicitness had only made it all the more intense. Justine knew how to please him and prided herself on the fact.

But Lynsey was in a little silo of her own amongst the Branch members. He confided in her with things he wouldn't even tell Justine, spent most evenings laughing and joking with her, treating her as though she were family. Literal family. And not once, since she'd rebuffed him, had he tried it on with her again. No consequences for her slight, just pleasantries. It made Justine want to smack the shit out of her every time she saw her sanctimonious face, but if she did that then the consequences would be severe.

"Well, she's obviously frigid so I'm not gonna waste my fucking time. You can sort her out. I think she's pissed the bed, anyway."

Justine stepped around Lynsey and left the room, neglecting to close the door on her way out. Alison was still struggling against her restraints, the altercation that had nearly taken place before her making her apoplectic with fear. It was one thing to be kidnapped by strangers, but another when your abductors began fighting over you.

"Don't worry about Justine," Lynsey told her quietly. "She has a huge chip on her shoulder with the words 'teacher's pet' written along the side. She'll calm down."

Sitting on the edge of the bed, Lynsey looked Alison up and down. "She was right about one thing though. We do need to get you cleaned up."

Alison strained to look down the bed. "I've pissed myself?" She let her head flop back onto the thin pillow and began to cry. Her sobs seemed to come from deep within her body, leaving her mouth in staccato gasps.

"I just want… to go home. I won't tell anyone, I swear. Joe and I weren't even that close, honestly. I only worked with the man. I won't call anyone. I just want to… go… home."

Lynsey gently touched her forehead. "It'll be okay, I promise. Let's get you cleaned up and get you something to eat."

As she left the room, Alison felt an uncomfortable calm wash over her. Was this it? Did she know she was going to die?

She had no idea what any of this was about, other than it obviously concerned Joe. She'd been telling the truth when she'd told them they hadn't spoken since he'd left the paper. As to why they wanted him, she couldn't even hazard a guess.

She finally began to feel the damp cold of the wet beneath her and her eyes welled up again. Alison tried not to chastise herself too much, despite the utter embarrassment she felt. *How odd,* she mused. *Embarrassed about that in front of your kidnappers.*

Taking a moment, Alison recognised a drowning depth of quietness in her surroundings. Having lived and worked where she had for so long, to be somewhere where the lack of noise was deafening appeared alien. It was as though there was a power, building but waiting to be unleashed, like a dam poised to burst its walls.

Lynsey re-entered the room with a steaming washbowl, clean bedding and what appeared to be fresh clothes. She placed the items on the chest of drawers and moved beside the bed.

"I'm going to uncuff you so you can freshen up and I can change the bed. Please, don't try to run, not because of me but because of them."

She nodded her head sideways towards the door. "They'll kill you, I guarantee it. I won't be able to stop them. If you do as you're told, everything will be okay, I promise. I know you have no reason to believe me, but it will. But for both our sakes, don't try to run."

Lynsey held Alison's gaze, as though trying to read her thoughts. After a few beats, Alison nodded slowly and supported her agreement with a quiet "Okay".

What other choice did she have?

'Plans are nothing; planning is everything.'

Dwight D. Eisenhower

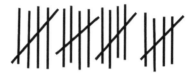

THE FORCE OF THE BLAST SHOOK THE WINDOWS.

Lamont had been prepared for it but it had still taken him by surprise. He looked around, confused at his surroundings, only to realise he'd tipped over in his chair and was lying on his side.

Joe, Heather and the two officers were on the other side of the room, having both been knocked back by the force of the blast. Screams and confused cries echoed around the building, interspersed with alarms blaring.

Lamont rose to his feet, his gait like that of a new-born fawn. He leant up against the wall beside him and took a few deep breaths. The ringing in his ears was nauseating. He'd expected something noteworthy but had to admit the force of the explosion had surprised him.

There must be nothing left of poor Rebecca.

He found himself wondering if she'd felt anything when the charge in her back had detonated. Heather calling out broke his musing. She was instructing the officers to find out what had happened and immediately stormed over to Lamont, her expression a mixture of confusion, dismay and full of fuck.

She grabbed him roughly by the arm and slammed him up against the wall with enough force to take his breath away for a couple of seconds. "What was that? Talk now or I swear I'll beat you to death in here and say you tripped. TALK!"

Lamont grinned crookedly. "That, detective, was the result of the device implanted in Rebecca's back."

There was a heavy silence between them, the only noise in the room Joe's grunting as he pulled himself to his feet and brushed the dust from his clothing.

"That doesn't answer my question," snarled Heather.

"It was a small explosive device, implanted under the surface of her skin."

Joe stepped closer and stood beside Heather. "Trust issues, much?"

Lamont chuckled. "It's not about trust, Joe. It's about power. Rebecca was special and volunteered. She was a true believer and now she's become…"

"A martyr," Joe interrupted. He fired a sideways glance at Heather, hoping his expression had said enough to concern her. It appeared to have done the trick.

"Why?"

"Why does someone climb a mountain? Because it provides a rewarding stimulus that reinforces behaviour. What do you hear around you?"

Heather frowned, trying to regain her composure whilst simultaneously doing as he asked. She heard screaming, crying, panic and confusion. At that moment, an officer burst through the interrogation room door, his black uniform now mostly grey from the dust and debris.

"Are you okay, Ma'am?"

Heather nodded. "We're fine, thanks. Could you send someone in here?"

The officer looked slightly frustrated at her request, as though she'd just added another job to what was probably an already huge to-do list. He nodded and closed the door behind him.

Heather turned back to Lamont, her arm still pinning him to the wall. "Enough games. Why do this?"

A smile, as brief as a passing shadow, crossed Lamont's face. "It's funny. All you have to do is something no one understands and they'll end up practically doing anything you want them to."

He let the silence build for a moment before continuing. "All around you, panic, chaos and turmoil. All your officers running around, wondering what just happened? Is it a terrorist attack? Where's Rebecca? I'm certain we left her in that cell somewhere. And of course, everyone will flock to this location – media, journalists, emergency services – and focus on this one event. This will be the most important thing to have occurred today. No one will be talking or thinking about anything else."

Joe sidestepped quickly to stand beside Heather. He had realised what Lamont had done, the cogs all aligning in that moment whilst he was spouting his riddles. How could they not have seen it?

"It's a distraction. Misdirection. He's done this to divert attention to something else."

"What are you talking about?" Heather snapped.

"Like he said, everyone is going to come here. They'll think it's terrorists or the I.R.A and all come here. And whilst you're all looking this way, there's something going on in the other direction."

"Like what?"

"I have no idea, but it won't be good whatever it is."

Lamont began to laugh. It was a low and guttural at first but quickly built to a raucous bellow. Tears formed in his eyes, prompting him to raise a hand and wipe them away.

"Are you insane?" Heather asked caustically.

Lamont sighed, a few tear trails still marking his face. "See, earlier you wouldn't comment on my mental state, but now you're asking me. However, in response to your question, I'm not insane in the slightest. It's just that tomorrow everyone'll be saying how this was the worst day in Irish history, which given your history is saying a lot."

"And?"

"And," Lamont replied. "To me, I'll just remember it as Wednesday."

Joe pulled Heather gently to one side, his voice barely a whisper. "We need to find out what he's up to. I have a friend who can help, but it means I'll have to leave."

Heather considered his request, occasionally glancing back

to look at Lamont. His face showed no signs of anxiety or concern. If she had to hazard a guess, she would say he looked… satisfied.

"Okay," Heather said flatly. "Do what you need to do. I'll lock him up if there's anywhere left to put him. But if you find anything out - *anything* - you call me, okay? I mean it, Joe."

He nodded and shot one last look at Lamont as he made his way out of the room. Joe's anger was slowly giving way to fear because he now realised that whatever they were up against had suddenly become much bigger.

He also had a terrible feeling that he would end up having to deal with it on his own.

'Denial, panic, threats, anger – those are very human responses to feeling guilt.'

Joshua Oppenheimer

THE PUBS IN TOWN WERE IN FULL SWING AS JOE MADE HIS way towards Sim's flat.

Traffic thumped around him, banging over the ubiquitous potholes in the road whilst the music from Doheny and Nesbitt's up the street drifted out and into the night.

Steam occasionally drifted out as doors swung open, the exiting customers ducking deep into their scarves as they stepped outside into cold air to smoke.

He smiled at two young girls as he walked past them, one returning his smile whilst the other sneered at him as though he were a pervert. Both girls had on skirts that resembled belts to Joe, with tops cut so low he was curious to know why they didn't already have hyperthermia. The reciprocative girl was still smiling, her expression provocative and which appeared to carry the promise to consciously and irrevocably fuck the shoes off his Irish arse.

As he moved past her and noted her tut at his apparent disinterest, he found himself thinking of Maxine. Why a stranger had made such an impact on him was equally as interesting as the *how* she'd made that impression.

He knew very little about her and could only take what she'd told him as the truth due to having no other option. And it all seemed a little too convenient. Or maybe he was just overly suspicious from his reporting days, Perhaps things were exactly as they seemed. But he couldn't shake the feeling that he was now on a lampless sea with Maxine being the tempest, pulling him further towards the eye of a hurricane that wouldn't be sated.

He knew he should get away, but like the sirens in the stories, she had a hold over him he couldn't quite understand.

Joe climbed the front steps of Sim's building wearily. He realised he hadn't slept for nearly twenty-four hours. With the adrenaline from the explosion at the station wearing off and the late hour, he knew he'd have to rest soon. Whatever he was getting into, he didn't want his attention compromised by a lack of sleep.

Sim buzzed him in without asking who it was. He knew she would have seen him on the myriad of cameras surreptitiously set around the perimeter of the building. The excited sounds of the evening faded away as he closed the door behind him and trudged up the staircase.

As he approached her door, he saw it was already ajar and could smell food in the air as he walked into her flat. "Curry?" he shouted into the empty room.

"Bombay Bad Boy Pot Noodle," came the reply from the

kitchen. "And keep your fucking voice down, you bell-end. Your girlfriend's asleep."

Joe quietly closed the front door and followed the sound of her voice, taking up a position against the door frame. "Why does everyone keep saying that? She's not my girlfriend. She's just…"

"I know, I know," Sim said derisively. "She's a friend who's a girl."

"Right," Joe agreed.

"So," she said whilst spooning a huge mouthful of noodles into her mouth. "What do you want at ridiculous o'clock?"

Joe made his way into the living room and threw himself down on the sofa. The lighting in the room was subtle, making him feel even more tired.

Passing traffic cast elongated shadows on the walls in the dim light, their tormented wraith-like shapes distorting as they made their way across the room. He found their monotonous presence soothing. Joe could close his eyes and happily sleep until tomorrow afternoon, but he needed Sim's help so rest would have to elude him for now.

"You heard about what happened at the station?"

"Yeah," came her garbled, food-masked reply as she followed him into the room and sat down in the chair opposite. "It's been all over the news. Every public sector service and media provider are there I think, along with Sky, BBC, RTÉ and most likely CBeebies. Aside from the big arse explosion, what actually happened?"

Joe ignored Sim's loud burp as she scraped the bottom of her Pot Noodle tub and placed it beside her on the table.

"I don't know for certain, but I don't think the explosion was the point. I think blowing Rebecca up was for something more than theatrics."

"She what now?" Sim said, stunned.

"Rebecca Sill? They blew her up. Well, the device implanted in her back was explosive, so it was probably on a timer or at least I hope so. If she wasn't on daylight savings, it's a bit of a bastard. But yeah, basically she martyred herself for some reason."

"Which was?" Sim asked, still visibly surprised at Joe's reveal. "I don't know, but I think it's a prelude to something else. Think about it. These Obadians now have most of the island focused on the bombing. All the usual theories will be floating about; terrorists, IRA etc. Until the Gardaí make a statement, it'll be supposition city. And whilst everyone is looking that way, I think they've got something going on in the opposite direction."

Sim snorted. "That's a bit thin, don't you think?"

"It's practically anorexic," Joe agreed. "But I have a hunch."

"Didn't Ciarán once threaten to cut your nuts off if you said you had a hunch?"

"No," Joe replied with a laugh. "He said I wouldn't get a job selling the Big Issue."

Sim smiled and acknowledged with a simple "Ah."

"He's right," came Maxine's voice from the doorway of the bedroom. She was wrapped in a towel but her hair was dry, telling Joe she was about to go in the shower or get a bath. He thought the time was unusual for that sort of thing, but what did he know? He couldn't remember the last time he'd had a shower.

"About the distraction thing. Did the explosion happen this evening?"

"Yeah, about an hour or so ago whilst I was at the station with your fearless leader." Joe pushed himself up from the sofa and walked to her side. "Why? What do you know?"

"Not much," she replied, unsecuring the towel and rewrapping it around her waist. Joe caught a glimpse of her taut midriff and breasts, the sight of which stirred a desire in him.

"Lamont always said there was a plan for a huge event, one that would get the world's attention and achieve in one go what took Stark so long to do. The murders so far were really just to test the resolve of the followers. They had to show they were up to the task. And he's not the leader."

Joe's jaw hardened. "What event?"

"I only know it was based around doing in one night what Stark had taken years to do and that someone special would help them achieve it."

"Does this mystery person have a name?"

"I've only ever heard him referred to as The Broker."

"That doesn't sound at all ominous," Joe said with a grimace. He looked over at Sim sitting at her computer, watching the conversation take place and caught the look in the eye. She was thinking the same thing.

Turning back to Maxine, Joe closed the distance between them. "How do you know all this?"

"I was with them a long time Joe. You learn things."

Tensing, he took a step back. "So, why didn't you mention any of this earlier or when we first met? You could have stopped Rebecca from dying."

"Listen, I didn't have to come to you at all," she retaliated, taking umbrage at his disapproving tone.

"So, why did you?" Joe said louder than intended.

"Because I knew only you could help me with what I need to do."

He clenched his jaw. She had him at a disadvantage insomuch that he knew so little about her he wasn't in much of a position to challenge her claims.

In an effort to minimise his implications, Joe stepped forward and wrapped his arms around her. "I'm sorry, Max. Rough night and a million thoughts running through my head. I didn't mean to imply anything. I guess he just got to me."

She returned his embrace, nuzzling into his neck so deeply he could smell her skin. He found himself lost again in thoughts of her body and how she'd made him feel the other night.

"Hey, I turned up on your doorstep and presented you with a boatload of problems," Maxine said. "I understand, I do."

She gently pushed Joe back and held him at arm's length. "Listen, I'm going to jump in the shower. You're welcome to join me."

"Thanks," he replied with a smile. "But I think I'll keep

Sim company. I'll borrow your towel though. My car hit a leprechaun on the way in."

Maxine smiled and ventured back into the bedroom, removing the towel just before turning the corner to allow Joe to catch a glimpse of her bottom.

"Wow, I hope you didn't pay much for that?" Sim said, breaking Joe's thoughts.

"Pay much for what?"

"The really short leash she has you on."

"Shut up," Joe snorted in good humour. He glanced back towards the bedroom, hearing the sound of water running. Satisfied they'd be uninterrupted for a few minutes, he moved quickly over to Sim and sat down beside her.

"How's your checking up on her going?" His voice was low, despite the fact he knew she wouldn't be able to hear him. "All of this is a little too convenient."

"Convenient because you got a shag out of it, or convenient because it's all a little… convenient?"

"The latter," Joe said with an air of annoyance in his voice. In sleeping with her he'd fucked up more than Donald Trump, which was putting it lightly. He just didn't need reminding of it right now. "She's hiding something."

"Let me guess," Sim said as she got up and walked over to her bank of computers. "Hunch?"

Joe smiled. "Hunch," he confirmed.

"Well," Sim said as she flicked on computer screens and various other pieces of equipment. "I'd trust your hunches more than most people's facts, every day of the week and twice on Sundays."

"Thank you."

"And in answer to your question, so far I have nothing, but I'm doing the same as before, last time took a piss detail."

"Excellent. I'd like full urinary depth," Joe chuckled. "How much longer do you need do you think?"

"For you, Joe I'll forgo all basic human requirements, such as sleep, eating, voiding my bowels…"

"All right, all right," he said. "I love you."

"Fuck off!" Sim replied and started tapping away furiously, running search algorithms and writing programs.

Joe walked to the front door and made his way onto the landing. He turned back as he was closing the door. "Tell Maxine I had to see a man about a dog."

"Uh uh," Sim grunted, her attention firmly focused on whatever she was doing.

Joe still didn't understand how she found out some of the things she had, but he knew she was a loyal friend. They'd known each other for more than ten years and though they hadn't always kept in touch as much as they should have; whenever they met again it was like he'd only spoken to her yesterday. That kind of friendship was hard to find and he had no intention of letting it go.

Closing the door, he made his way back outside. The streets were fairly empty, most of its future occupants, power drinkers and trustees of modern chemistry in the pubs and bars, most likely oblivious to what had occurred earlier and to the very real risk that perhaps death was stalking some of them.

A game had been set in motion. A game of chance involving a group's obsession with a serial killer and their desire to show the world just how easy it was to take a life.

Stark had been right when he'd said that humans were just cattle - all their lives they were fattened, inoculated and herded for the sole purpose of pursuing an agenda known only to a precious few. Like the Obadians.

Or The Brethren.

Joe recalled Lamont's fascination with wanting to know what had happened on the night of Stark's execution. The realisation of what he was going to do made him feel nauseated, but despite his reservations, he knew there was no choice if he was to get answers. Heather would be too preoccupied dealing with the fallout from the explosion and the death of a prisoner in her custody. He'd keep her in the loop as and when he could. But for the moment he knew he was on his own.

It was time he paid The Brethren a visit.

'Misdirection is the key element. We can create a space where we give them something to look at to take their mind away from what they really should be seeing.'

Chris Conti

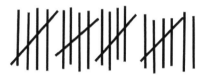

Lamont couldn't help but smile at the amount of effort they were putting into his transfer.

He was sitting in the back seat of a car slowly moving along sparsely-lit country roads. One of the officers kept glancing back through the metal grille separating them, staring at Lamont with blank, cold eyes. Lamont simply returned his thousand-yard stare with a smile until he would turn away.

The cuffs were linked by a short chain, something he could have easily picked given the motivation. He just knew he didn't need to. He'd be free soon enough.

"Who's this lunatic?" one of the officers exclaimed, pointing towards the windscreen.

About twenty yards ahead a woman was standing in the middle of the road. Petite and pretty with long blonde hair and a short chequered blue dress, she looked like one of the cast from *Little House on the Prairie*. Only the knee-high boots cast her in a twenty-first century light.

The glow from the streetlight beside her accentuated the perfect symmetry of her face. To the officers in the car, she seemed on edge or high on nervous energy. Whatever the reason, it wouldn't matter in about twenty seconds. The weapon swinging by her side confirmed the theory.

Although the pump action shotgun contained only five rounds – one already in the breach – she wasn't concerned about needing more shells. If she couldn't bring them down with five shots, then she didn't deserve to live.

The officer in the passenger seat had just begun to say that he'd step out and address her when the windscreen on his side of the car exploded inwards in a flurry of glass. Lamont ducked down behind the chair to avoid flying shards which were accompanied by blood and brain matter.

The second officer barely had time to call out before the girl was standing by his window, the shotgun chiming as it touched the glass. She smiled sweetly as she pulled the trigger, the side of his head and most of his face being blasted off. His body spasmed gently whilst it fell to the side and over onto his colleague on the passenger seat.

The girl stared at the body until the twitching stopped before turning her attention to the prisoner in the back. She skipped happily to the rear door and pulled it open, still brandishing the shotgun.

Lamont shuffled out and stretched as he stood, breathing in the night air. He held his hands out in front of him, prompting the girl to immediately step forward and pull something from her hair. Five seconds later, the hairgrip had freed Lamont who threw the handcuffs in the back of the car and shut the door.

"My dearest Angela, pleased to see you again. Thank you so much for that. Granted you could have picked a more desirable location than the middle of nowhere to mount your little rescue, but that's just me being picky. Do you happen to have a handkerchief?"

Angela fished a piece of muslin from her pocket and spat on it before handing it to Lamont. She stepped on her tiptoes and kissed him on the lips as he vigorously rubbed the areas of his face splattered with human viscera. He threw the cloth on the floor and massaged the reddened areas of his wrists where the cuffs had been before letting out a huge sigh.

"You should keep those," she said, nodding towards the back seat. "We lost the last set."

"Now, now dearie. Stay focused. We'll have plenty of time for that later. For now, I wish to know if everything is in place."

"I believe so," Angela replied, playing with fingers on his left hand. "The last of them were being delivered as I left. Justine was organising them all. O'Connell's bitch is secured and everyone's ready to follow your orders."

He acknowledged her enthusiasm with a nod. "We are close, my dear. But there's still one more piece of the jigsaw we need before our task is complete."

"You're placing an awful lot of faith in that man," Angela said with a sneer. "How do you know he can be trusted to do what you need him to?"

"Because dearie, the lengths a man will go to in order to protect those he cares about is often amazing. Joe won't only do it for his colleague; he'll do it because he needs to know how the story ends. It'll eat away at his conscience and pull at his pride. He needs to know what we're doing this for, otherwise, he'll never be at ease."

Angela remained silent, accepting his explanation. "How far away is the car?" Lamont asked, noting the great masses of clouds reflecting the moonlight as they moved across the heavens.

"Five minutes walk."

He took Angela's hand and headed in the direction she'd gestured towards, the pendulous clouds cracking open and forcing cold, merciless rain down upon them.

The heavens knew tonight would be a night no one would forget. Lamont could feel it as they blessed them as harbingers of an obliterating storm.

'When one with honeyed words but evil mind persuades the mob, great woes befall the state.'

Euripides

THE RHYTHM OF THE RAIN HAD ACTED AS A SEDATIVE, despite Alison's abject terror at her situation.

Lynsey had changed her bed whilst she'd stripped, washed and dressed in the dry clothes she'd brought her; white socks, linen trousers with matching blue shirt. Hardly her usual Top Shop fare, but given the circumstances she wasn't going to complain.

A cup of coffee and some sandwiches had been left for her on the chest of drawers, brought in by a woman who went unnamed and looked as though Alison's very presence there was a personal insult to her.

Wherever *here* was.

She'd heard what sounded like a commotion whilst eating her food before drifting off into a fitful, exhausted sleep. Alison was terrified beyond anything she'd ever experienced before, but prolonged fear had the unfortunate side-effect of being draining. She didn't want to close her eyes, afraid of what might happen but found it impossible to stay awake. After spending a few minutes sobbing and talking to God in an incoherent babble, Alison had tried to compose herself.

After taking deep breaths she'd managed to stop hyperventilating and had relaxed back onto the bed which is where sleep had slipped its inky fingers around her weary mind and lulled her towards its embrace.

———

She dreamt she was drowning, the pressure of the water around her a crushing weight on her chest and yet her body felt dry. She frantically tried to swim to the light she saw above her. The agony of her running out of air was overcome by the instinct not to breathe. She fought her way to the surface, ignoring the searing pain in her lungs.

Alison knew how it worked when you were drowning. Too much carbon dioxide and too little oxygen would trigger chemical sensors, leading to an involuntary intake of breath. The breaking point. Hold your breath, you'll die, breathing in might not kill us, so we'll take a shot at it. Sebastian Junger called in 'voluntary apnoea' in his book *The Perfect Storm* about the fishing boat, the Andrea Gail.

Alison's brain was screaming at her to breathe, her arms and legs pushing against the force of the water around her but she couldn't get any closer to the surface. Her mouth felt wet as though something was being forced in. The weight on her chest shifted slightly and she could breathe once again. Her body was tingling as though being caressed by many hands, her legs being parted as she swam up and up but never reaching the light beckoning to join it.

Alison woke with a start as she felt something between her

thighs and saw Justine's head positioned there. She immediately pulled her body back to put some distance between them, horrified at realising what her dream had actually meant.

"Oh no you don't," said Justine, pulling Alison back down towards her by the legs.

She kicked out, catching Justine a glancing blow to the side of her head. It had the opposite effect than the one Alison had desired, instead making her more aggressive in her attempts to reposition Alison where she wanted her.

"Tonight's the night. I might not get another chance at this, so you're going to be my last supper, so to speak."

"Get the fuck off me!" screamed Alison, hoping that Lynsey would hear. That anyone would hear.

Justine pulled her further down the bed and wrestled with her legs, trying to secure them with the handcuffs she'd brought. Alison wriggled and thrashed as hard as she could, raining blows down on Justine's face and head to no avail.

A hand lashed out and caught Alison across the side of her face, stunning her. Momentarily dazed, she lost a few precious seconds which was all Justine needed to ensure Alison's legs were cuffed and spread apart. She quickly moved up to the head of the bed and tied Alison's hands together, binding them to the bedhead.

A rough hand forced open Alison's jaws and shoved a rag into her mouth before Justine stepped back and dusted her hands off as though she'd just finished a hard day's labour. "There we go," she said mockingly. "All positioned and ready. Lamont would kill me if he knew I was doing this, but he won't know, will he?"

Alison's sobs were barely audible through the cloth in her mouth, her eyes wide in horror.

"No, we won't tell him, because if you do I'll gut you, you fuckin' slut." Justine climbed onto the top and positioned herself over Alison, their faces almost touching. Her breath smelt of stale cigarettes and alcohol, causing Alison to wretch behind the gag.

She licked Alison's face and slowly worked her tongue down her neck before repositioning further down between her legs. Justine gave her a sly wink before ripping down the linen pants and forcing her face between her legs. Alison bucked and wrestled against the restraints while Justine's hands pinned her down by her calves. She could feel Justine probing with her tongue, the sensation making her feel sick.

Closing her eyes, Alison silently prayed; for help or for death she wasn't entirely certain. Kidnapped, drugged and now being sexually assaulted because of her association with Joe O'Connell. How the fuck had her life ended up like this? What was he involved in that could possibly require her to suffer like this?

She began to breathe rapidly, quickly becoming dizzy. The faster she inhaled, the dizzier she found herself becoming. Alison's peripheral vision began to surrender to the encroaching darkness around her as she felt Justine's tongue violate her over and over again. She felt as though she was staring down a long, black tunnel, the light behind her dimming with every passing moment. The sound of the door being flung open and slamming into the wall beside it brought her back to the now.

Justine leapt from the bed as Lynsey flew at her, grabbing her by her red hair and swinging her around and into the chest of drawers beside the bed. Wobbling to her feet, Justine wiped the blood from her nose where her face had been stopped by furniture. "You fucking, stupid bitch!" she snarled. "You're fucking dead!"

She charged forward, only to be greeted by an elbow to the side of her head as Lynsey pivoted around. A short, hard blow, but it had the desired effect, causing Justine to collapse to the floor like it had just given way beneath her. She was breathing but not moving.

Satisfied she was unconscious, Lynsey moved quickly to Alison's side and pulled the rag from her mouth before untying her, all the while encouraging her to remain quiet. She knew she'd made enough noise already, but Lynsey hoped the laughter and celebrations taking place further down the hall regarding their success this evening would be enough to mask what had just occurred. Asking Alison to remain quiet was more to give her something to focus on, rather than their talking being heard. This would only work if she was somewhere remotely near calm.

She fished about Justine's person, searching her pockets for the key to the handcuffs. Satisfied she had it, she turned her attention back to Alison.

Alison's gaze was fixed, her lips moving silently as though whispering to someone unseen. Lynsey acted quickly, untying the ropes securing her hands and the cuffs on her feet. Lynsey sat her up and looked her up and down, searching for any signs of injury. Seeing none, she looked into her eyes and caressed her cheek whilst gently calling her name.

"Alison. It's okay, it's over."

She continued to mutter silently, her eyes reflecting the chilling bleakness that was her situation.

"We have to go, honey. We can't stay here."

Still getting no response, Lynsey gently lifted one of her hands and kissed it. "We have to go, Alison. Right now. I can get you out, but you have to help me. There's no time. If they find us, we're dead." Alison's gaze slowly shifted towards Lynsey, her face remaining expressionless but she managed a nod. Lynsey smiled and gently helped her to the edge of the bed. "Can you stand?"

Again, another nod. They took a few steps towards the door before Alison stopped. She began trembling, tears welling but refusing to fall as though awaiting permission.

"I don't know if I can."

Lynsey looked at her sadly, wanting to put her arms around her. "I'm scared too, shitless in fact. But we have to go and now. He's coming back right now and take my word for it, we do not want to be here for what happens next, never mind when Justine wakes up." After a few moments' contemplation, Alison began to move again slowly, as though sleepwalking. As they approached the door,

Lynsey turned towards Alison. "Ready?"

"No."

"Me neither. Let's go."

She opened the door and peered down the corridor. The sounds of her companions celebrating echoed off the walls, loud and excessive. Satisfied they were alone for the moment, Lynsey firmly gripped Alison's hand and pulled the door behind them, leading her in the opposite direction to the noise. They passed the kitchen to their left and then turned right into the long part of an L-shaped corridor, their quick movement causing the wooden floorboards popping and creaking beneath them. The sound was deafening, even though Lynsey know no one would hear them at the other end of the house.

Heading in the other direction would have been quicker, but there would have been no way they'd get past the others without detection. At least this way they should be able to get away without incident.

Lynsey put her back to the wall and encouraged Alison to do the same, edging out to the corner. She leant around to look ahead. The hallway leading to the back door was deserted. Not wishing to linger in the hallway longer than necessary, Lynsey gently pulled Alison towards her and together they quickly moved down the hall. At the bottom, she positioned Alison against the wall and watched as she slid to the floor.

"I'm okay," she said, sensing Lynsey's concern and holding out a hand in a dismissive gesture. "I just need a moment."

Leaving her to rest, Lynsey positioned herself in front of one of the two windows by the door and peered outside. Ahead the sky was dark, but to her right, the horizon was a mixture of yellow and orange as it burned away the dark, neon-blue of night. For a moment, Lynsey saw hope trying to tear through darkness. She hoped it was a good omen.

She signalled to Alison but when she didn't respond, went and sat down beside her. They didn't have long, but she needed her to be independently mobile.

"How you doing?" She tried to keep the impatience in her voice to a minimum. "Ready to go?"

Alison's face looked gaunt in the dim light, her eyes red and sunken. "Why are you doing this to me?"

Lynsey thought carefully before answering. "Because they're bad people, about to do some very bad things. They needed something from O'Connell and wanted to use you for leverage. That's all."

"That's all?" Alison said, her voice rising. "I've been kidnapped, drugged, almost raped and all you have to say is 'that's all'?"

Lynsey stared down towards her feet, ashamed of her part in Alison's kidnapping. She didn't know what else to say.

"So why are you helping me?" Alison asked suspiciously.

"I need to be out. It's gone too far and I don't want any part of what they're doing, but you don't just leave The Obadians. And I couldn't live with myself if I didn't help you. Call it atonement."

A flicker of recognition at Lynsey's comment flashed over Alison's face. "Obadians? As in Obadiah Stark?"

"The very same," she replied, standing and hoping the hint would be apparent.

Alison nodded wearily, too tired to ask her to elaborate and held out a hand. Lynsey helped her to her feet and once satisfied she was steady, moved her to the door to stand alongside her before making their way outside.

Their transition from the house to the other side of the yard that led into a wood went unhindered. Alison noted the unkempt garden and dilapidated shed before lifting her gaze to her surroundings. The building behind them was huge, ornate, with sash windows and peeling cream brickwork. It looked Victorian, certainly a period house, but she failed to recognise it. She'd been hoping to see something that would give her an indication as to where they were, but there was nothing except the white plumes of breath coming from her mouth in the cold morning air and the mosaic of shadows and sunlight interlaced on the ground.

"We need to climb over here," Lynsey said, pointing at the fence. "Then we can make our way through the woods. The caravan park is just across those wetlands. We should be able to rest there for a while."

Alison wheezed a weary "Okay" and moved over to the fence where Lynsey was already positioned to give her a boost over the top. Lifting her as high as she could, Lynsey saw her disappear over the top and heard a dull thud on the other side. She whispered for acknowledgement and upon hearing it, took a few steps back before running towards the fence and using it to propel herself to the top and over. Nodding at Alison, they quickly made their way forward into the woods.

The shadows grew deeper as they ventured further in, the sun finding fewer and fewer places to intrude. Lynsey found herself feeling anxious, unable to stop her heart from beating hard and fast. Their adrenaline-fuelled escape had masked the fact that she knew they would come looking for them and would be unyielding in their pursuit. So they needed to ensure he couldn't find them.

With Alison stumbling along beside her, Lynsey felt cold.

Nothing but a deep, all-pervading cold.

'I ask you to judge me by the enemies I have made.'

Franklin D. Roosevelt

GIDEON ARCHARD SAT BEHIND HIS DESK IN HIS TOP-FLOOR office on Grafton Street, just along from the very exclusive Westbury Hotel.

Light and spacious, climate-controlled, Joe found himself surprised at the tasteful decoration as he was escorted in by the attractive, young lady who'd introduced herself as Emily at the front desk. He wasn't certain what he'd expected from the décor, to be honest. Given what he knew about Archard, he would have guessed black walls with pentangles plastered all over them and chicken entrails on tap for those last minute conjurings.

He felt surprisingly calm as he was shown to one of the two seats in front of the large desk. The last time he'd seen the man before him, he'd been threatened with death if he ever spoke about what he'd seen involving them and Stark. Now he was here, about to ask him for help. Which meant asking The Brethren for help, by proxy.

Archard acknowledged Joe's presence with a smarmy smile showing too many bleached teeth and hastily ended his telephone conversation. Replacing the receiver, he reclined back in his leather chair and clasped his hands together. It was all Joe could do to not leap from his seat and smack him in his arrogant face.

"Good morning, Joe. What a pleasant surprise, truly. It's lovely to see you."

The door behind Joe opened, allowing a big man with slicked back hair and a black leather jacket entrance. He walked with a slight limp, carefully positioning himself over the seat in the corner of the room before relaxing into it.

"You remember, Mr Milton," Archard indicated towards their new addition to the office.

Joe turned and looked at the man in question. "Son of a bitch!" He exclaimed. "How's the knee?"

"Ah, yes, of course," Archard said. "Milton has you to thank for the limp. Not very generous given he was assisting you with your flat tyre."

Joe snorted. "Whilst trying to kill me. The A.A's recruitment process must have gone to shit."

"Ah, you still have that dry wit that proved so popular."

"And you're still a smarmy fucker, so some things never change." Archard's smile momentarily faded before he cleared his throat.

"So how can we help you today? Do you have an injustice you wish us to investigate on your behalf." His tone was once again cordial, his smile as enticing as a piranha.

"What do you know about someone called The Broker?"

Archard frowned, the lines in his forehead making him look like a Klingon. His grin never wavered. "Nothing. Never heard the name before."

"How about Lamont Etchison?" This time Archard's smile faded.

"How do you know of Lamont?"

"He kidnapped a friend of mine and then turned himself into the police, whilst claiming he was responsible for the recent murders."

"The Branch Obadians," Archard acknowledged. "We've been aware of them for some time. They have a fascination concerning your old friend, Mr Stark. He's something of a deity to them apparently."

Joe shook his head. "He's more than that. He's their inspiration."

"Inspiration to do what?"

"Something terrible," Joe said after a thoughtful pause.

"I don't see how any of this is my concern," Archard replied with an air of irritation. "We're a multi-million euro business, Joe. We deal with miscarriages of justice, humanitarian causes, carry out a lot of philanthropic work…"

"…have your fingers in every political pie from here to China, manipulate the banking industry when you feel like it, have key players at the highest levels of power across the world and won a humanitarian award," Joe interjected. "Yeah, I know all about you. I said I wouldn't share what I knew. You didn't tell me I couldn't investigate."

"Touché," Archard said with a conciliatory nod. "But that still doesn't explain why you asked to see me. We're not friends, Joe. We're not enemies. We're, let us say, at opposite ends of the morality spectrum."

"Who is he to you?" Joe asked.

Archard wouldn't look Joe in the face, instead wiping his hand across the top of his desk as though checking for dust. "That isn't important," he snapped.

Bored with Archard's posturing, Joe decided to take the upper hand. "I was told to tell you that Lamont has Subject One's journal." The colour drained away slowly from his face and he began to fidget slightly, his brow beginning to bead with sweat.

"He told you that?" Archard clarified with an audible swallow.

"Yup," Joe said nonchalantly.

"And did he say exactly what it was he wanted?"

"He asked to know what you did with Stark's body after the execution. Sorry, I meant murder."

"Murder? Come now," Archard said, still flustered at Joe's revelation. "He was a serial killer, responsible for the deaths of twenty-seven women that we know of. You can't tell me you feel sympathy for him?"

"Not sympathy," Joe said when he replied. "Empathy. Whatever you did and wherever he was in his mind when you had him sedated, he saw something… learnt something that was incredible. A murderer learnt how to feel remorse, or at least understand what it was. Don't you see how important that is? You should be using that information to treat people like Stark, not as a freak-show demonstration of your power."

When Archard spoke, he looked as though he were making an effort to choose his words carefully. "Your opinion is inconsequential in the matter. I know you'd love to shout from the rooftops about the irony of what we do – the company who fight for injustice are purveyors of injustice themselves – but the fact is, aside from yourself, the only people who know what we do in respect to that side of our company are the people who work for me. And trust me, they'd never say anything."

"Afraid for their lives, eh?" Joe asked, receiving only a shrug from Archard in response. "But as it happens, you're not entirely right about that. Someone else does know."

Joe waited a moment, purely just to see the look on his opponent's face before continuing. "Etchison knows."

"That's not possible, he was never…" Archard cleared his throat and wiped the moisture which had accumulated on his top lip. "There's no way he could know what happened that night."

"Yeah, he knows 'cause I told him," Joe said with a slight air of misplaced guilt. He didn't feel bad for The Brethren or the man sitting before him, but having said it out loud, he had an uncomfortable feeling of having betrayed a confidence.

Archard's eyes narrowed. "You told him? What you saw that night?"

A muscle flexed in Joe's cheek. "Don't worry, I remember what you said to me, tell anyone and you're dead etc, etc, but I really had no choice. As I said, he kidnapped a friend of mine, someone I used to work with… someone I used to care about and said I either find out what happened to Stark or she dies. Of course, I couldn't tell him what happened to his body, as by that time you'd sedated me… again."

Archard looked over towards Milton with an expression that must have meant something as he immediately rose from his seat and left the office.

Joe sat in the prickly silence, wondering if he'd just signed his own death warrant. Archard had risen from his seat and was standing by the window, gazing out across the Dublin skyline.

The Halfpenny and Millennium bridges were sparkling in the morning sunshine, the reflection of the River Liffy giving them a bejewelled appearance. The Dublin Spire, standing as a memorial to Horatio Nelson, watched over the city, always a reminder of the bombing in 1966 by members of the IRA that had destroyed the former Nelson's Pillar which had originally stood there.

"Who would believe him?" he asked without turning around. "He's a member of a crazed cult obsessed with a murderer."

"People don't have to," Joe replied assertively. "Whatever their plan is, if it's successful they'll get the attention they want, for their cult and once again, Obadiah Stark. Then they'll start spouting what they know and though many will see it as the ravings of crazy obsessives, some will ask questions and that kind of attention is something you could do well without if you want to carry on your quest for global domination."

Archard turned and faced Joe, his weighing up of the

consequences visible on his face. His words had acted like a tranquilliser dart, silencing him as he considered his options. Joe saw it as an opportunity to keep pushing.

"Look, I don't like you or what you stand for," he stated, gesturing around the room as an indication that his statement meant the company. He seemed to be struggling with the words he was about to say, as though his throat had gone into spasm. "But I need your help. He was being transferred last night to Shelton Abbey Prison, which I know is shit as it's minimum security but there's nowhere else to put him at the moment. They were going to provide a special detail of officers to keep him secured once he arrived there. We need to go there and you need to tell him what happened to Stark's body."

Joe could see Archard ruminating over his suggestion, but also knew he wasn't convinced. He wasn't going to risk his entire livelihood, company and arrest for something as trivial as Joe's asking for help. He needed to appeal to his vanity.

"Look," Joe said, moving to stand beside Archard. "You claim to stand for those who've suffered injustice. I have a strong feeling people will die if you don't do this… Alison will die if you don't do this. Look at the publicity you can get from assisting the Gardaí in this investigation. Think of the headlines. 'BRETHREN C.E.O SAVES LIVES OF… WHOMEVER IT IS LAMONT IS POSSIBLY GOING TO KILL.'"

Archard frowned at him.

Joe continued, waving his hands dismissively. "It doesn't matter about the headline, the fact is that you can get some publicity from this which will be unique. You could even get another humanitarian award… you know, if all the members of the Elie Wiesel Foundation have a stroke."

Archard looked as though he was about to speak when Milton burst into the room, looking anxious. He nodded to his boss, implying whatever he had to tell him was private. "No, go ahead," Archard said. "It appears Joe O'Connell and I have a mutual interest."

Milton looked unimpressed with the news of a temporary amnesty but moved closer before speaking.

"Lamont Etchison escaped from custody in the early hours of this morning. His whereabouts are currently unknown."

Archard cast a chilling look at Joe. "So, how does this affect your grand plan?"

Joe couldn't quite comprehend how he felt at that moment. He spoke the only word he could think of that would perfectly sum up his thoughts at hearing Milton's news.

"Bollocks."

'The only person you are destined to become is the person you decide to be.'

Ralph Waldo Emerson

|||| |||| |||| |||| ||||

THE LIGHT BURNING IN THE LARGE LIVING ROOM CAST THE omnipresent shadow of Lamont on the wall behind him.

He and Angela had driven carefully back to the house after his escape, aware of the need to remain inconspicuous. The authorities would already be alert to what had happened and would be searching for him with all the resources they had available. However, he also knew that those resources would be limited due to the explosion earlier that morning so they still had time.

Granted, the plan had sounded too far fetched when he'd heard it, with too many variables that could bring it screeching to a halt, but she'd persuaded him he had to have faith that it would work. *'Small gestures hold little sway; big ones all are unable to ignore.'* He guessed that was true. Certainly, after tonight, no one would be able to ignore what they'd done.

Arriving home, both he and Susan had been greeted with embraces and welcoming comments by the Obadian

members. Some commented on how they'd been worried
he wouldn't make it back for this evening's event, others
just telling him they'd never doubt his return. Now, with
the remaining members in his thrall, Lamont felt a power
like no other coursing through him.An energy he knew the
others in the room felt.

Conviction.

"Some would say we've drunk the Kool-Aid, jumping on
the bandwagon of those before us and that we're only a
carbon copy of the Charles Mansons' and Jim Jones' of
the world. But we're not – we are more than they ever were
and soon, more than they could have ever imagined. We
built up our family from nothing. We didn't need drugs to
keep you believers. We didn't need sex to make you
submissive. Those were the mistakes others made, using
chemicals and coercion to ensure fidelity to their cause.
You stayed because you believed the world needs to
change. There are nearly 7.4 billion on the planet, but only
twenty make it turn. Jamie Dimon, Ali Hoseini-Khamenei,
Jeff Bezos, Mark Zuckerberg, Gideon Archard… these
individuals and others have used their multi-billion pound
conglomerates to slowly pervade our lives with their
brainwashing social media apps, control over money and
the consumer industry. They have made us believe that
they are benevolent and that all they do is for the greater
good. But we know this to be an untruth. All they have
succeeded in doing is allowing people to become
subservient to them and blind to the truth. They are part
of the Global Elite, their goal to turn the world into a
fascist state. United Nations, International Monetary Fund,
C.I.A, the Bilderberg Group, all have deceived us and
continue to do so by stealthily introducing global
capitalism.

"David Icke sees the truth, not with his claims of the
Babylonian Brotherhood but with his understanding of the
law of attraction; that good and bad thoughts attract
experiences. That is what brought us together, my friends.
Shared experiences and beliefs. If we don't act then
darkness and evil will roll over and consume the earth. We
need to take a stand and make a statement and show that
Rebecca and Susan's sacrifices were not in vain. Therefore
tonight, we shall show this country and the world that
Obadiah Stark's message lives on. That those who think
they have all the power have none, that it lies with us
instead, the people. Tonight, we will make reality once
again Stark's glorious twenty-seven and remove those
whose arrogance has blighted this world from the face
of it."

The room crackled with energy, the individuals before him
ready to do what was required of them. He scanned their
faces, taking in their expressions of excitement and
apprehension. It was almost tangible, something he could
feel energising him and making him feel as though he was
approaching his destiny.

Yet there was something wrong that he couldn't quite put
his finger on. An impalpable acknowledgement that
something wasn't right. Lamont signalled to Angela who
was engaged in what appeared to be a heavy conversation
with one of the members.

She approached him slowly, making certain he saw the
sway of her hips. She curtsied before him in mock
deference. "Ma Lord."

"Where's Justine?"

Angela shrugged. "She's not here?" she replied, looking around. "I don't know then."

His eyes blank, Lamont gestured towards the door. "Please go and fetch her, dearie."

She nodded without umbrage at his instruction and weaved her way between her fellow family members before disappearing from the room.

Lamont still couldn't shake the feeling he had – not foreboding. Presentiment. That despite all the planning which had gone into this evening, there was an anomaly that couldn't be accounted for. An incongruity that could destroy all they'd worked to build.

He heard Angela shouting before seeing her appear in the doorway, supporting Justine with an arm around her shoulder. Her face bloodied and bruised, she stared at Lamont with anger in her eyes. Not anger at what had happened to her, but specifically directed towards him.

"What happened?" he asked sternly, making his way towards them both.

"Your favourite pet," Justine hissed venomously despite the slurring of her words. "She happened. Traitorous bitch. And she took your leverage."

"How long ago?" he demanded.

"A couple of hours," Justine said, wincing in pain from what he suspected was a fractured or broken jaw, given the swelling around the side of her face.

Lamont's eyes darkened. "And no one noticed they were gone? No one heard anything?" He span around and glared at all of those in the room. "NO ONE HEARD ANYTHING?"

Silence fell like an anvil, everyone suddenly staring at Lamont and over at Justine, confused at to what had just promoted his outburst and why a colleague was injured. Justine didn't reply to his question, her response simply a look of defiance.

Lamont pushed past them and out into the hallway. He paced for a few moments before turning his attention back to Angela.

"This changes nothing. Everything will go ahead as planned. Do you understand?"

Angela gave a slight nod of acknowledgement. "What about Justine?"

"Get her fixed up," he replied, his voice dripping with disappointment. "I imagine our Lady will want to speak to her later."

Lamont walked away swiftly and made his way downstairs to the basement. There was no sound. He hadn't expected to hear anything as he knew they were all sedated, but still knowing there were 19 people down there made it an unusual experience.

A mixture of men and women, all wearing whatever they'd been dressed in when taken. Some had on suits, others t-shirts and tracksuit bottoms. One woman was in her nightgown and another had obviously been going on a fancy dress night out given she was wearing a Pink Ladies jacket and had her hair in a tight perm.

He stepped carefully over their prone bodies, checking a few of the shackles securing them to the wall as he passed by. Everything seemed in order. The Broker had done well, though Lamont had expected little else given the money he was being paid. He was glad he hadn't been here when the delivery had been made.

Lamont had only met The Broker once before but had taken an instant dislike to him. There had been an uncomfortable vibe surrounding him and pulsating off him in waves. It had reminded Lamont of the devices you put in your garden to repel cats that give off an ultrasonic sound that only the cats and certain people can hear. Lamont had always been able to hear them in his mother's garden and it had always made him wince as though it were penetrating his very bones.

That was how The Broker made him feel. Chilled to his very marrow. He'd always felt he could just laugh in the face of death if he ever came across it. But that man.

His was the face of death.

'Man is not what he thinks he is, he is what he hides.'

André Malraux

THE RANGE ROVER SWUNG LEFT ONTO THE R445 AND continued towards Kenmare.

Joe stared out the window, catching sight of the Pfizer pharmaceutical building in the distance. He knew the Oral-B headquarters were over there somewhere too, along with the Department of Defence and Lily O'Brien's Chocolate factory. Medicine, mouths, secrets and sugar – key elements that made the world go round.

He made a mental note to look into the history of his country a little more when all this was over. Joe realised he'd been remiss in giving her the attention she deserved, having always been preoccupied with work or drinking.

The voice of his old schoolteacher popped into his head, telling him that Newbridge used to be part of the USSR and that they had strong, historical links with Russia. He remembered that the most notable, aside from the rumoured agreement between the IRA and Stalin, was that Limerick native Peter Lacey who, as Russian Army Field Marshal Peter Petrovich Lacy, had participated in the battle of Poltava where Peter the Great had defeated the army of Charles the Twelfth.

A country steeped in fascinating history, yet here he was sitting in a vehicle with an odious individual who probably wouldn't give a crap about nostalgia unless there was money to be made in it.

Acutely aware it was a four-hour drive back to the station in Kenmare, Joe considered just jumping out onto the motorway now and leaving Archard to explain his death to Heather. A painful, gravel-filled wounded suicide would be preferable to sitting next to the man who Joe was fairly certain matched the definition of a cockwomble.

"So, you no longer work for the paper?" Archard chimed up after having been silent for ten minutes.

"You know I don't," Joe snapped. "What was the point in working for a media outlet when you can't report the news?"

"You think anyone would have believed you if you'd told them what actually happened that night? To Stark? About Vicky and her sister? Despite our insistence that you leave well-enough alone, you had no evidence so would have succeeded in causing only chaos and delay to the process."

"Chaos and delay?" Joe repeated snidely. "Who are you, The Fat Controller? What you were doing was wrong, irrespective of whom it was to. You don't get to make those decisions about life and death. You're not God, you're just a rich idiot on a power trip, hiding under the guise of benevolence. Besides, it's not me you have to worry about now, it's your old friend, Lamont."

"Old friend?"

"Oh, come on," Joe said with a laugh. "I used to be a journalist. He worked for you, didn't he? He worked for you and he did something or saw something or knew something he wasn't supposed to and you got rid of him."

Archard's jaw clenched, allowing Joe to see he'd hit a nerve. "Lamont Etchison was once a member of The Brethren. He, along with myself and four others, refined the ethos behind the company and what we wanted it to represent moving forward, at least to the public. It was markedly different from that of my great-grandfather who'd founded the company, but as with all things you have to change with the times. Back then it had been politicians, government officials and socialites on the board. As you know, you need qualified, experienced people running a company, not just friends who are only friends because they borrowed your lawnmower ten years ago."

"Ploughshare," Joe said.

"What?"

"They won't have had lawnmowers back in your great-grandfather's day. It'll have been a ploughshare."

"Right," Archard replied with irritation at Joe's patronising response. "Anyway, Lamont had… contacts in some of the more clandestine elements of the government who offered to provide us with more funding if we agreed to continue running a project parallel to the work we were doing regarding the justice system."

"What project?"

"You know what project," he confirmed. "You were there."

Joe sat in silence, processing what he was hearing whilst hoping there would be more. He had a funny feeling that what he was being told was not only incendiary but also his death warrant being signed. But he knew Archard wouldn't do anything yet. He needed Joe, at least for the time being, so he had time to think of something that wouldn't involve his death.

Archard took Joe's silence as an opportunity to continue. "I'd had it shut down after they arrested Gary Ridgway in 2001 for the Green River killings. It was too expensive to run and as we couldn't do anything with our findings, it seemed to be a fruitless venture. But Lamont convinced me, alongside his promise of funding, that we should reactive it. Stark was coming to what we now know was the end of his reign, so he seemed like an ideal candidate to start with. In fact, he was the perfect candidate."

"For what? What were you doing and what does this Subject One thing mean?" Joe's voice had begun to rise, both with confusion and frustration.

Archard let out a sigh. "Subject One was the individual the project started with, a man named James Maybrick."

Joe repeated it a few times to himself quietly. "Maybrick, Maybrick… why do I recognise that name?"

"Because he was Jack the Ripper," came the matter-of-fact response.

Joe blinked in surprise. "Excuse me?"

Archard continued staring at the road ahead, but his expression appeared far away. "My great, great-grandfather, Sebastian Archard, who formed The Brethren, had an… arrangement with Maybrick. His crimes brought about civil unrest and political opportunities that Sebastian knew could be exploited in order to put him and his partners in positions of power in the Government. Once there, he was able to expand the company and ensure that he was able to deal with the largest corporations and businesses in the world. He took it from a small, twelve-person secret group to a multi-million corporation which funds healthcare, pharmaceuticals, liquid fluoride thorium reactors to counteract global warming…"

"… all built on the acts of a madman," Joe countered, realising the fragments of research he'd received from Kev had been correct. The Brethren had known the identity of Jack the Ripper. Worse than that, they'd been working with him. "You still haven't told me what you were doing with these people… what you did with Stark."

"That's not important," said Archard irritably. "What is important is that Lamont claims to know about Maybrick's journal which contains details regarding The Brethren's involvement with him. And if he shares those details, they'll draw unnecessary attention I would rather avoid."

Joe knew there was more to it all. Archard was hiding something and it was big. He was just about to question him further when he felt his mobile vibrate in his pocket. Issuing an apology, he fished it from his pocket and looked at the screen.

Sim.

"Hey, you. What's up?"

"Where are you?" She sounded concerned, anxious.

He glanced over at Archard. "I'm just on my way back to

Kenmare. I have someone who might be able to help us."
There was no response.

"Sim? Is everything okay?"

After a few beats, she began to speak though her voice
remained tinged with nervous energy. "You know you
asked me to look into Maxine for you?"

"Yeah. Is she there?"

"No," Sim replied with an air of relief. "She went out a
few hours ago. Anyway, I found out something that I think
you should know. It's big, Joe. I mean, it's really fuckin' big
and I'll be honest, I'm shit scared."

"Why? What is it?" The anxiousness in Joe's voice
promoted Archard to look at his passenger with a puzzled
expression.

"You told me she'd said her parents were dead. Well, that's
not entirely true. Her biological mother died when she was
seven, but her foster parents, the Gregory's are still alive."

"Okay, she didn't mention them. Still, that's not unusual.
I'm a virtual stranger to her, so perhaps she didn't want to
share personal stuff like that?"

"Personal stuff?" Sim snapped. "But she was happy to fuck
you? How much more personal can you get?"

"All right, all right. Sorry, go on." Joe heard her let out a
groan. "Anyway, I managed to trace her birth mother's
death certificate… a lady named Erica Fenton. She
worked in a bar in '85 in New Orleans and moved here
in '97 with her two-year-old daughter, one Tracy
Fenton."

"Okay, so far so normal. So, she has a sister," Joe said,

gazing idly out the window at the encroaching darkness threatening to envelop them.

"No, you're not paying attention. There was no one named as the father, only her mother's name – Erica Fenton, nothing else anywhere. So, having a funny feeling akin to your gut about her, which F.Y.I I've had the entire time, I decided to dig a little deeper as you know I can and I managed to get hold of an online copy of John Franklin's report, you know, the one he conducted not long before Stark was executed."

"I know, I read it, but I still don't see where this is going Sim," said Joe impatiently. "What's the Franklin report got to do with anything?"

"Well, I'm fairly certain you didn't see it all," she replied smugly, her anxiousness momentarily replaced by excitement.

"What do you mean?"

"Sections of it were sequestered after the interview under the pretence that they would 'potentially cause anxiety to person or persons named therein.' Basically, they didn't want the public to know."

"Know what," asked Joe, getting an uneasy feeling in his stomach. Lamont continued to glance over at him intermittently, trying to work out what the one-sided conversation was about.

Sim's voice rose as she spoke. "The reason I'm shitting myself. I don't know why I ever let you get me involved in this. I knew it was hinky the moment you showed up with her, you bastard."

"Simmy!" Joe shouted. "Know what?"

"Know that Stark had a child…a daughter. Tracy Fenton changed her name to distance herself from her biological parents."

Joe let the phone drop from his ear slightly. Stark had a child? Impossible! How could he have not known? Then again, if you'd discovered you'd given birth to the world's worst serial killer's kid, would you want to tell him?

Shit.

"Joe? Are you there? Do you know what I just said? She changed her name to Maxine Groves. Maxine's his…"

The line went dead as though suddenly cut off. Joe checked to make certain he had a good signal. Three bars. He redialled her number but got a busy tone. Calling once again, Joe felt sick as a metallic taste began to coat his tongue. He could feel his heart rate increasing, his lungs seemingly unable to fill with enough air despite the fact he had all the air he needed around him.

"We need to take a detour," Joe said urgently.

"Why?"

"Because I think my friend's in trouble… big trouble."

"What was she saying?" Archard asked, his tone blasé.

"Something terrible," Joe replied thoughtfully. "But we need to go and now."

"Why should I care what happens to your friend?" Archard asked icily.

Joe turned in his seat to face him. "You should care because whatever she was going to tell me had something to do with the reason we're on this unpleasant road trip, so if you're happy not knowing whether or not it's something that could completely fuck up your life, fine. You can let me out here and I'll make my own way. And by the way, this shit is probably happening because you fucking removed notes from the Franklin report."

"Excuse me?" Archard said in an indignant tone.

"Don't you fucking dare. Only you would have had the power and the necessity to take them out because what they apparently held would have been a major fucking spoke in your wheels. Stop the bastard car!"

Archard looked at Joe and then the road a number of times, processing the options. It was already all getting out of hand. Could he really risk not knowing the information Joe's friend had discovered?

"Where are we going?" Archard asked, his tone filled with annoyance at being temporarily at the whims of his passenger.

"Dublin."

As Archard mumbled under his breath, Joe turned back to look out of his window. Though there was no rain lightning had begun to score the sky whilst thunder pealed in the distance. Joe thought it apt.

Whatever had been rumbling towards him from the moment he'd sat in front of Rebecca Sill would soon be making its presence known.

A sinister sepulchral storm that would be unrelenting.

'The high destiny of the individual is to serve rather than to rule.'

Albert Einstein

THE BRANCH OBADIANS MADE THEIR WAY DOWN THE STAIRS to the basement, single file.

Lamont had spoken to each of them individually, more to ensure they were not shaken or perturbed by the incident with Justine. He remained angry that no one had been able to intervene in stopping one of his own, his most trusted member, escape with his leverage. He realised he should have made better preparations perhaps instead of taunting the Gardaí, but it mattered little now. Everything was in place and there was nothing that could stop it.

Let Lynsey tell O'Connell or the authorities what they knew. By then it would be too late.

Joanne Charlton, one of the Branch's earliest devotees, had kissed Lamont on the cheek and taken hold of his hands, thanking him for the opportunities he'd given her and for the chance to be part of something historic. He acknowledged her words and told her what the repercussions of what they were about to do would echo for decades to come. She would be remembered.

Moving through the followers, he'd spent a few moments with Louise Hunter and Beverley Brown, both of whom were the Branch's most recent additions. They seemed jubilant and excited about what was about to take place, speaking of legacy and how Obadiah Stark's vision had been ahead of its time.

Lamont felt pride and simultaneous disappointment. Lynsey had been with him since the beginning and, despite the fact she'd refused to be involved in his larger plan, had proven herself invaluable. Her ability to procure martyrs to their cause had been exceptional, though in hindsight he recalled the last one she'd brought him – Catriona – had promoted something he could only define as remorse. He'd seen it in her eyes fleetingly when delivering her. Thinking nothing of it at the time, he'd simply thought it a remnant of her previous life. He himself had occasionally experienced melancholy at what he'd lost but had reassured himself that it had directed him towards a greater destiny. He'd have to ensure her punishment was fitting for her betrayal.

They would find her.

The Broker would find her.

Casting aside his thoughts for the moment, he made his way behind the last of his family and down into the basement. The Obadians had each taken up positions in front of the still unconscious nineteen individuals, kneeling before them in reverence. They were about to make a great sacrifice, one which Obadiah himself would have been proud of. It was only right that they were given due deference. He would ensure they were awake for it, of course. He needed them to know, see the fear and look of eternity in their eyes before they died.

Lamont collected the black case from the table in the corner and opened it in front of the person nearest to him, Julie Spindler; quiet and unassuming yet completely devoted to him and his beliefs.

She cast her eyes over its contents, pausing at the instrument similar to a Heretic's Fork. Removing it from its moulding, she turned it over in her hands, the polished steel glistening in the bright overhead strip lights. Smiling in satisfaction at her choice, Julie nodded at Lamont and he moved onto the next one.

He'd spent a lot of time collecting various devices that were functional but had personalities all their own. Some, like the Heretic's Fork, were an indulgence, the others a mixture of scalpels, long serrated knives and scythes. He had imagined it being almost biblical, with classical torture devices such as the Judas Cradle, Choke Pear and Scaphism being used, but it was difficult to find anything akin to longboats nowadays and as for the diarrhoea and insects…

Besides, she'd instructed him to keep it simple.

He checked his watch whilst continuing to part with his gifts.

It was almost time.

She would be here soon.

'We can easily forgive a child who is afraid of the dark; the real tragedy of life is when men are afraid of the light.'

Plato

JOE CONSIDERED THAT SOMEONE MIGHT BE ON THE OTHER side of the door.

It was there in the pit of his stomach, clawing at him, screaming for him to turn around. That if he ventured through the door, he would only find torment. But Sim was only involved because Joe had dragged her in, so it was on him to do what needed to be done.

He placed his hand on the door, took a few deep breaths and burst through, stumbling over the chair just inside. His heart was pounding, his eyes darting around the room at overturned furniture and smashed computer screens.

He stepped carefully between broken glass and shattered ornaments, making his way towards her bank of now-destroyed computers. He wondered if she'd managed to leave any notes, something that might give him an indication of what she'd been about to tell him.

Archard had been overly compliant at Joe's

recommendation that he remain with the car, not wishing to be involved with anything illicit. He'd found that statement amusing, given that he was one big ball of a bent bastard.

He cast his eyes quickly along Sim's desk space but saw nothing that he thought could help him. He was just turning back towards the kitchen when his phone rang.

Unknown number.

"Hello," he answered tentatively.

"Hi Joe," came the sound of Maxine's voice. "Sorry to bother you at such an inappropriate moment, but it seems that my plans for a slow reveal ala Arlington Road have been scuppered, so I'm having to accelerate things."

"Maxine? Or should I call you Tracy?" Joe said, caught off- guard at her phone call.

A long, intense laugh came down the receiver. "I prefer Maxine actually. I've grown quite attached to it."

"Let me speak to her!" he demanded.

There was a commotion and some shouting before Sim's voice came through the receiver. "I'm sorry, Joe," she said sadly. "I should have been more careful. I told you she was bad news."

"Simmy? What's going on? Are you okay?"

"She's fine," came Maxine's voice once again, having taken back the phone. "However that sentiment won't last long unless you do as you are told. I know you have Archard with you."

"How…?" Joe began to ask.

"Don't bother," Maxine interrupted. "Just trust me when I say I know a great many things, one of which is you need to bring your sexy butt and his corrupt arse to the location I'm going to text you, just in case that lovely, lady detective of yours is listening in. You and Archard will come alone or your computer hacker extraordinaire dies horribly. And believe me when I say horribly."

Joe sat down on the sofa behind him, struggling to process everything he was hearing. He felt like the wind had suddenly been knocked out of him, taking him by surprise and leaving him little time to prepare himself.

"What's this all about, Maxine? Why take Sim? You have Alison."

"Ah, well best-laid plans and all of that. Alison was assisted in escaping us. I hadn't seen a betrayal coming, so my bad. Sim is her replacement and a good thing too. She's a bit of a blabbermouth."

"I still don't understand?"

"You will," she replied with an air of conceit. "Check your phone in a moment. And Joe… don't try to grow a brain. It doesn't suit you."

The line went dead, leaving Joe with only the sounds of cars passing by outside and a distant chime of music in the air. The hood of night had fallen over the city, leaving him with only, once again, a woman on his mind and uneasiness in his heart.

He felt his phone vibrate and checked the message that appeared. *Glendalough. Prophet House.*

Rising with a sigh, Joe pinched the bridge of his nose and

slowly made his way back to the car, but not before securing Sim's door as he left.

Stepping into the night, the buildings around him reflected the lights of the evening's unfolding festivities whilst people went about their business, oblivious to the darkness that existed in their world at this very moment.

For a moment, it was easy to believe that all was right with the world.

'Some of the biggest cases of mistaken identity are among intellectuals who have trouble remembering that they are not God.'

Thomas Sowell

The air was filled with murmured voices praying to God for help and cries for mercy.

The nineteen individuals were in various states of alertness, some wide awake and screaming, others still somnolent but roused enough to know that they were somewhere terrible where something horrifying was about to happen. A few were pulling frantically at their shackles, hoping they'd break. They wouldn't of course. Where they all were was a place with nowhere to run or hide.

Lamont had gathered all his followers together in a circle around him. Their heads were bowed as though in prayer, uttering thanks to him and to the one they were here to honour.

He wondered how Obadiah would have felt, knowing that he had inspired so many to carry on his work. Joe's claims that the man had undergone some sort of epiphany prior to his death were ridiculous. Lamont knew that a creation such as Obadiah Stark would have never lamented his life. Frankly, he found it insulting that O'Connell had suggested such a thing.

Lamont heard the creaking of hinges as the door to the basement above was opened. Some of the whimpering ceased as though they were expecting salvation to be visiting them in the darkness. A soft scraping of footsteps down the wooden stairs was accompanied by a woman's voice, hurling insults to whomever she was with. Lamont smiled as he saw Maxine emerge with the source of the colourful metaphors.

"So pleased you could make it, Lady Groves. We were just about to get started. And who is this, may I ask?"

"This," Maxine replied, throwing Sim roughly to the floor, "is the substitute leverage to replace the one you so carelessly lost."

Lamont felt his face begin to burn. "I sincerely apologise for that, my Lady. Such a lapse shall be dealt with, I give you my word."

"I don't want promises, Lamont," Maxine snapped back. "I want results. We need to do this and quickly. If your traitorous bitch and that woman have made it to the police which, let's face it is where they'll have gone, then everything we've worked for all these years will be ruined. We need this done and now."

Lamont nodded his understanding. "And O'Connell?"

"Don't you worry about him," Maxine replied with a pretentious smile that betrayed innocence. "He'll be here soon."

"Because of her?" he asked, nodding in Sim's direction.

"Because of her," Maxine acknowledged.

Sim pulled herself upright and stood defiantly. "You're all fuckin' crazy, you know that, right? I thought I'd seen the bottom of it, but then you bring me here and there's a crazy underground basement filled with more fuckin' crazy. And you," she shouted, pointing at Maxine. "I never fuckin' liked you. Joe and his dick, it always gets him into trouble. First Vicky Carter and now you. Fuckin' Obadiah Stark, you just can't get away from him no matter how much you try."

"Nor should you try," Maxine said in a soft voice. "I'm proud of who I am."

"Whatever," Sim fired back. "You keep taking those tablets."

"Such ignorance. But you'll see soon enough." She signalled towards Lamont. "Restrain her. She can watch and think about what'll happen to her when we're done."

"Yes, my Lady."

He grabbed hold of Sim by the arm and dragged her towards the set of restraints in the corner of the basement. Fighting and swearing, she struggled against his hold all the way. A kick to his side resulted in a backhand across her face, subduing her enough for him to secure her in place.

Looking up, Sim spat out blood that speckled his shoes. "It'll all fall apart, you know."

"Really? And why is that? Lamont asked lazily, his eyes filled with righteousness.

"Because you have the one thing that all others before you

have had that was their undoing… arrogance. Once you
think you're too clever to be caught, you're usually already
fucked."

Lamont's focus never left Sim. Though his gaze was
pinned on her, he was looking beyond and inward, as
though what she'd said had given him momentary pause
for thought.

"We'll see," was his defiant reply as he turned and rejoined
his brethren for what was to come.

'Lands of great discovery are also lands of great injustices.'

Ivo Andric

GLENDALOUGH (GLEANN DÁ LOCH) COUNTY
WICKLOW, IRELAND

Archard had parked in a private lane leading to the residence, overlooking a field of long grass.

The harvest moon hung low in the sky, silently watchful over the large house he and Joe were approaching. In the distance, the hills formed large, geometric shapes, silver in the moonlight. A cascade of stars peppered the sky, looking for all intents and purposes as though God had pricked holes in the blanket of night.

Joe found himself remembering constellations from his childhood and found the recall comforting, though it soon dissipated when his mind snapped back to the task at hand.

They were making no effort to hide given Joe's invitation from Maxine. Archard had wittered on about his reputation and that of his company, but he knew as much as he didn't want to be there, the details Lamont had about him and The Brethren were too important to be ignored. He needed to find a way to ensure he kept his silence.

The house had looked inviting at a distance; gabled and brightly lit. It was only as they'd moved closer that it had taken on an altogether foreboding appearance. Stepping onto the porch, floorboards creaking beneath their feet, they looked at each other in silent agreement before Joe opened the door. The sudden warmth caused them both to shiver due to the change in temperature, Archard moving in front of Joe so he could close the door.

They stood for a moment, heads cocked, listening carefully. Tense. Except the wind whistling through cracks in the windows and the sound of a clock ticking loudly, the hush was eerily deep. It had more character than Joe had expected. Despite the thin layer of dust that appeared to coat everything, there was no mess and everything looked neat and tidy.

Joe took the first step, aware of the blind corner ahead and the casting of his shadow on the floor. They hugged the wall and turned right, following the corridor along to a bedroom containing an unmade bed and a chest of drawers on an angle.

Joe moved closer to the bed and picked up one of the handcuffs secured to the frame. He looked over at Archard who simply shrugged, instead moving a little further down the hallway and out of Joe's line of sight. He wondered if Alison had been kept here.

As he turned round he saw blood soaked into the carpet, not a large amount but definitely signs of a struggle when taken into account with the off-set chest of drawers. Did they still have her?

He tried suppressing feelings of guilt at her having been

drawn into all this along with the tide of adrenaline he knew was making his heart race.

Joe stepped out of the bedroom and followed Archard's path along the hallway. Boxes and plastic storage containers were stacked along each side of their path, filled with what looked like tins and packets of dried food. He guessed it was stock for the people who lived here – the Branch Obadians.

He considered that what they were doing was ludicrous. Two of them entering a house, albeit invited, full of potential murderers. An invitation didn't necessarily ensure their safety, especially as it had come from a woman he now knew was crazy. But what choice did they have?

They'd taken Alison and Sim, dragged him back into a life he'd been trying to forget on his own terms and had then piqued his journalistic curiosity, damn them.

Joining Archard in the kitchen at the end, he was about to say it was too easy and ask why they hadn't seen anyone when he felt his phone vibrate in his pocket. Signalling for him to stay put, Joe ventured back towards the bedroom and stepped inside, closing the door slightly to dampen any noise.

"Hello," he said in a voice slightly above a whisper.

"O'Connell?" It was Heather. "Where are you?"

"I'm… following up on a lead."

She gave an audible sigh. "Joe, what did I say to you? No more secrets and bullshit. Where are you?"

He clicked his tongue against the roof of his mouth

thoughtfully. "I'm at the Branch Obadian compound, house, whatever you want to call it."

"And you're there why?" Already he could hear the annoyance in her voice.

"Look, it's not what you think. I got a phone call from Maxine…"

"The woman you kept secret from me?" Heather interrupted. "That's the one. She's his daughter, Heather. Stark's daughter. She called me saying that she had a friend of mine and that if I didn't come she'd be killed."

He could hear a door open and an increase in the noise level at Heather's end. "Jesus Christ! And you slept with her?"

"Really, you want to do that now?"

"Okay, okay. Well, you'll be pleased to know we have another friend of yours here…one Alison Clime. She and a Branch member were picked up by some of my men after making a phone call, saying they'd just escaped from somewhere we might be interested in knowing about. I'm guessing it's the same location you're at."

Joe let out a sigh of relief. "Alison's there? Is she okay?"

"A little worse for wear, scared and tired but otherwise she's fine. The doctor is just with her now. The Obadian with her rescued your friend as she wanted nothing to do with what they had planned."

"Did she tell you what that was exactly?"

"Nope, not yet. She's in The Box at the moment, so no doubt we'll get it, hopefully with less explosive results than the last one."

Joe found himself surprised at Heather's attempt at humour. "Things any better there?"

"Chaotic," she said calmly. "Quite a few were injured, no one except the suspect killed, thank God. Going to need a shitload of screen doors and a good renderer, but other than that we'll keep on ticking."

Joe opened the door slightly, checking Archard was still where he'd told him to wait. Seeing him sitting at the table, he stepped into the middle of the room. "Listen, we're at the old abandoned house in Glendalough. You know the one?"

"Yeah, I know it. Are you there alone?"

"Not exactly," Joe said tentatively.

"What does that mean?"

"It means I haven't got time at the moment, just get as many people as you can and get here fast. I don't know what's going on, but it doesn't feel right. Get here, Heather. Get here soon."

Sensing his desperate tone, Heather's voice softened. "I will, Joe," she said as reassuringly as she could. "Just stay out of sight. We're on our way."

The phone went dead as Joe placed it into his pocket and headed back towards Archard, the preternatural silence unnerving. He moved around the corner and found himself looking at Maxine who had a knife gently resting beneath Archard's throat.

"I thought that was you, creeping around." Her voice was cheerful and light. "This is just perfect."

Joe moved slowly around the table and sat down opposite

her, his hands coming to rest on the surface in an act of submission. "Why are you doing this? You need to help me understand."

"Oh, you'll understand soon enough, lover. And I can't wait to see your face when all the pieces drop into place."

Realising any attempt at mediation or escape was futile, Joe silently acknowledged his situation. Even if he did run and leave Archard, which wouldn't be the worst thing to have on his conscience, he didn't know how many of them were in the house. It wasn't worth the risk, given Heather was on her way.

"So," Joe asked genuinely. "What happens now?"

"Now, you accompany me downstairs and get to watch the festivities. This will be historic, Joe. I'm so glad you were able to make it."

"Make it? I didn't get the impression I had a choice. And speaking of which, where's Simmy? Is she okay?"

Maxine gave a tut of disappointment. "Joe, what do you think I am? She's safe... somewhere. Whether she remains that way and in one piece is entirely up to you. As for forcing you to come here, you're splitting hairs – blackmail, willingly, what's the difference? All that matters is that you're here."

He found himself slightly sickened by the clapping of her hands together in excitement, knife and all before she gestured for Archard to stand.

"My right-hand man and your former employee has some questions for you."

Taking up a position behind him, Maxine turned towards Joe. "And you, come on. You don't want to miss this."

"I can't believe I slept with you," Joe said with as much disgust as he could muster.

"Oh, come now. It was great and you know it. The illicitness of it all, the feeling of being dominated… fancy a second go? I'm certain I can fit you in."

"Not a chance," Joe replied with a sneer. "Shame about Alison, eh?"

Her face momentarily lost its composure at his snide comment, her eyes taking on an altogether dark hue. A single vein popped out on her forehead. "It was, but then I think we ended up with a far more suitable substitute. I mean, she found out all about me which makes her interesting."

Maxine's smile returned and she indicated for Joe to move ahead of them both. Anger rising in his gut from her cavalier response, Joe did as he was instructed. He spoke as he moved passed Archard.

"You're quiet all of a sudden."

"What's there to say? I want to get out if this alive if I can. If that means doing what I'm told, then so be it."

"Guess this scuppers your plan for killing me then, eh?" Joe stated as they made their way down the wooden treads that squeaked with every step.

"I don't know what you mean," Archard said in an unconvincing tone.

"Come on, I'm not stupid. You tell me all your secrets and were just going to let me go? Well, I guess you won't have

to get your hands dirty after all. I have a feeling this lot
much prefer unsanitary digits."

Archard grunted as the last step brought them all into a
windowless vestibule. Just ahead Joe saw multiple people
secured to the wall, each of them with another individual
by their side softly chanting under their breath. He
couldn't make out what they were saying, but didn't think it
was "I'm going to let you go in a minute."

Taking up a position against the wall beside them, Joe and

Archard watched as Maxine took up a position in the
centre of the room, her arms outstretched.

"Gentlemen, now that you're here we can begin."

'Et tu, Brute?'

William Shakespeare

THE NIGHT SKY WAS ABLAZE WITH THE STROBING RED AND blue lights from the cars.

Heather was shouting instructions to the men from the Emergency Response Unit in the back of the van with her, aware that Alex would be reiterating the same to the men in the vehicle behind them.

"This is potentially a hostage situation. We've been informed by a member of the Obadians that up to fifteen or more civilians may be at the house, being held under duress. In addition, Joe O'Connell and an as yet identified other are also there. This is why the bombing earlier - it was a diversion to facilitate a mass kidnapping. All corporate types, rich and powerful, though not necessarily likeable. Nevertheless, we need to be fast, quiet and quick, so check those corners and make certain we bring them all home in one piece. Expect the suspects to be armed and consider them extremely dangerous. We know what one of them was able to do whilst in custody… take nothing for granted. Any questions?"

She was met with a cascade of shaking heads and mumbled nos. "Let's get this done and stay safe."

The driver shouted through the grille that they were less than ten minutes away as Heather checked her ASP 21, the extendable batons that were introduced in 2007.

She glanced at the men around her from the armed unit and felt a pang of jealousy at their being able to carry a weapon, immediately admonishing herself for thinking it. No officer outside of Northern Ireland carried a gun and that was how it should be.

Hopefully, there would be no need to use them.

Joe and Archard had been positioned at the rear of the room to allow a vista of everything around them.

Joe felt like a naughty schoolboy, being told to stand in the corner as punishment. Or maybe that guy at the end of The Blair Witch Project. Either way, they'd understood that if they didn't do what they were told then they'd be killed. He wasn't entirely convinced that was the case.

Maxine and Lamont wanted them to see what was about to occur; to show off the way criminals do. If they were going to die, it would be afterwards, but hopefully Heather and the cavalry would be here by then… hopefully.

Sounds of people in terror filled the room, though it had become more muted due to the sheer exhaustion of being consistently scared. Maxine had disappeared somewhere and returned a few moments later wearing a long, flowing black dress and high heels. "I always like to dress for the occasion," had been her statement.

After consulting quietly with Lamont and a few of the Obadians, she'd taken up a position in front of them all that demanded their attention.

"Tonight we embark on an epic journey; the accumulation of many years' hard work. The cattle before you are individuals who represent some of the one-percent in our country, having made a living earning money and rising the societal ladder at the expense of others. Eight have already fallen. These remaining nineteen will be your doorway to a higher level of being. Do not fear what you are about to do, fear what will happen to the world if we do not. *He* had a vision for the world, a realisation that all you needed to do to disrupt the natural order of things was to introduce a little chaos. Show the politicians and government officials that real power is not given, it is taken. What we do here will shake the country to its very core. It will show the heretics and disbelievers that all you need to do to make a change is to have a small number of dedicated individuals who possess a strong belief in your cause.

"I remain grateful for your loyalty. You have followed Lamont's teachings well, as he has mine. Now is the time to do what must be done and honour *his* memory. The twenty-seven."

"The twenty-seven," they all repeated in unison.

Heather and the Emergency Response Commander surveyed the grounds surrounding the house.

He was using night-vision goggles; she was using her eyes. He flipped them up and nodded at Heather, indicating it looked clear. The green fluorescent glow from his I.R equipment gave Halliday a sinister look as though he was about to Hulk out.

Signalling towards his men in the two vans parked further up the dirt road, Heather heard a barrage of footsteps approaching behind her. She found it comforting knowing that she was entering this unknown situation with some of the best men in the force. The men and Alex arranged themselves around her, taking up crouched positions to make themselves less visible. Halliday indicated for Heather to speak.

"We know from the member who escaped earlier today that they're planning a mass execution of the individuals kidnapped today as part of a ceremony. The plan is to take the suspects alive and ensure we bring all the civilians out safe and sound. Commander?"

Halliday flattened out a 2D schematic of the house and directed his penlight towards it. "Myself and Atkins will enter here," he said, pointing towards the front door. "The rest of you take up positions in a perimeter. No one moves until my say so. Is that clear?"

His men murmured agreement in unison before falling out in a two by two formation. Heather stepped closer to the Commander and motioned towards Alex to join her.

"So, this is it?"

"Nervous?" he asked in a flat tone.

"A little," Heather replied. "I haven't been in the field for some years, so I'm worried I'll be a little rusty."

Halliday gave her and Alex a thin-lipped smile. "The both of you just stay behind us and you'll be fine."

They took up position following him and Atkins in single file, Alex occasionally glancing behind them to make certain there were no surprises. She heard a voice come over Halliday's headset. "Commander, we've taken up positions around the house. Waiting your command."

"Acknowledged. Approaching the front of the house now."

Halliday hand signalled for Heather and Alex to stop as they mounted the porch, the floorboards creaking under their combined weight. Atkins took up position beside his commander.

"Tango One, we're entering the house now."

"Acknowledged," came the crackling response.

Opening the door slowly, the creaking of the hinges sounding like a howler monkey, they entered the house and stood still a few steps in. They heard very faint sounds of whimpering and voices from somewhere further inside the house.

A hand signal instructed Heather and Alex to enter and they began moving forward slowly, hugging the wall before pausing at the corner. Their tactical lights cast misshapen figures on the wall and floor around them, making them appear more like spectral wraiths than officers. Heather found herself momentarily fascinated at how the images twisted and distorted, almost as though they were telling a story of something long past. Or yet to come.

Passing what appeared to be a bedroom, mostly likely the one that Alison had been held in based on her description, and moving forwards they entered a kitchen area. Heather and Alex carefully checked their surroundings for any clues that may prove useful in regards to a prosecution case. Noticing a door behind them, Heather tapped Halliday on the shoulder to draw his attention to it. She wasn't certain if he had replied and she hadn't heard him or whether he had ignored her.

"Tango One, move in on my position. Middle of the house, kitchen area."

Once again, a muffled acknowledgement came over his headset. A few minutes later the remaining ten men appeared in front of them, their poise relaxed but certainly not complacent.

"Okay, Atkins and I will proceed through the door behind us, the rest of you take up position here." He gestured around the kitchen area. "You two," he said, pointing at Heather and Alex. "Stay here. We'll let you know when it's safe to follow."

Heather nodded, annoyed that they had to wait, but pleased that he hadn't been ignoring her. Halliday and Atkins steadied themselves in front of the door before counting to three quietly.

Halliday slowly made his way down the stairs, closely followed by his partner, their flashlights off to maintain an element of surprise and because there was enough ambient light at the bottom for them to see their way.

There was silence for a few minutes before Heather heard Halliday's voice calling to her and her Alex. His tone was riddled with what she could only describe as disbelief.

"You two better had come down here."

Reaching the bottom of the stairs, Heather and Alex saw a scene that they both knew would haunt them for the rest of their lives.

'Bird or beast upon the sculptured bust above his chamber door, with such a name as 'Nevermore'.'

Edgar Allan Poe

FEBRUARY 27TH 20:51

GLENDALOUGH (GLEANN DÁ LOCH) COUNTY WICKLOW, IRELAND

THIRTY MINUTES EARLIER

"NO!" Joe cried out as the lady with the Heretic's Fork forced her victim's head down in a swift, violent motion.

The prongs penetrated through the side of the woman's face, splintering her cheekbone and reappearing through her left eye. The bottom half of the fork sank deep into her sternum, accompanied by screams of agony that seemed to slowly taper off as though she were a machine, winding down. Vitreous fluid spilled out from her shattered eye socket and penetrated breastbone.

As she crumpled to the floor, Joe could see the red nail varnish on her hands. It appeared fresh as though she'd been getting ready to go out prior to being taken. The woman who'd committed the act, fell to her knees with her head in his hands as though asking for forgiveness.

It only took Joe a moment to realise it wasn't repentance she was pleading for; it was salutation.

Archard had turned his head away upon realising what was about to occur and hadn't opened his eyes since. He was giving off a low moan as though in pain, though Joe knew it wasn't discomfort he was feeling, it was fear.

One by one, Maxine instructed each of her followers to attack the person in front of them. The bodies fell like broken mannequins, some with their heads caved in at the side from repeated hammer blows, others falling to the ground as they tried to hold the lengths of intestines that had been released from their body using a knife. One man, whilst begging for his life had his throat cut mid-plea. Arterial blood sprayed everywhere, splashing across Joe and Lamont and covering the Obadian so completely he looked like an advert for a Grand Guignol caricature.

He carried on flailing at his face with the blade, pulling the man closer towards him and slashing away part of his cheek and exposing the bone. Once his face was a mass of bloody tatters, he let the man drop like a dead weight, the exertion of his efforts audible via deep laboured breaths.

Another had a short-lived look of bemusement on his face as a scalpel entered his stomach with the ease of a blade cutting butter. Again and again, the woman holding it sliced into his belly, spurts of blood flying from his body. After what seemed like minutes, his restrained body keeled over, convulsing for a moment as his innards splashed onto the floor like a length of sausages. He hit the floor with a wet thud and was still.

"JESUS CHRIST, FOR FUCK'S SAKE STOP!" Joe shouted.

Archard was retching, still refusing to view the horrors taking place.

As though under subliminal instruction, the Obadians began to file out of the basement, pulling down their dresses and tops to reveal the tattooed gravestone on their backs to Maxine as they passed. She placed a mark in the epitaphic on each member and they made their way up the stairs in single file. Some had a number of tallies, on others Maxine's mark was their first. None of them spoke, simply looking as though they hadn't a care in the world.

Only one person remained tethered in the basement, the most horrific part of it being that she'd watched all their fellow captives slaughtered and knew what was going to happen. Her pleas and fight for mercy and escape had all but left her through enervation and despair. She knew there was no hope, her only desire that it be quick.

"Why?" Joe asked Maxine as she moved back into the centre of the room. He was fighting back emotion as he spoke. "What for?"

"People like Lamont ingratiated themselves with the powerful and wealthy like your friend beside you. For money, for influence, it makes no difference. But watching over it all, I knew you could never trust those people, people like Archard, to shape the world the way it has to be shaped. The light, Joe, doesn't dictate history. It's defined by darkness. My father knew it, that's why he embarked on the journey he took – to show the world that the power they think they have is an illusion. True power lies in the hands of the faithful and the visionary."

"Your father," Joe repeated, a numb feeling beginning to envelop his body. His mind raced, processing hundreds of scenarios whilst trying to deny what it now knew to be true.

"I guess it must be in the genes," Maxine said with a smile

akin to a crocodile's as she stepped towards the remaining captive.

Gently caressing her head, Maxine knelt down so they were eye to eye. "Please don't cry, you're doing something wonderful for the world. I know, I know, seeing your kind fall around you must have been hard. The suffering of strangers always is. But know they died for a cause, as will you. Your gift will become part of the song at the centre of the world, one that will echo throughout history and force humanity to face the secrets of its own dark heart."

Maxine whipped a knife out from beneath her dress and deftly ran it across the woman's throat. For a moment, nothing happened except a slight change in her expression.And then slowly, as though being unzipped, a crimson line began tracking from one side of her neck to the other. Her head flopped back widening the gap in her neck to the point it resembled a fish's mouth.

Maxine stood and turned around as the body slumped to the floor and a soft thud. "Never gets old," she said gleefully.

Joe spoke through gritted teeth. "So, Lamont was just a misdirection? You were in charge of them all the time… guiding, instructing, but why the deceit? Why not just kill me or him?" He nodded towards Archard.

"Oh, you silly boy," Maxine replied with a hearty laugh. "I don't want to kill you." A look of relief drifted over Joe's face before Maxine continued. "But I do want to you suffer. How that torment will transpire, I haven't quite decided. I do have an idea, however."

"Do you care to share it?" Joe asked nervously.

"Nope," Maxine responded flatly.

"And who is this Broker?" Joe asked with as much defiance as he could muster.

"Honestly, I don't know. No one knows his name. He's the one who procured all these fine people you see around me." Maxine wafted her hands around the room at the mutilated corpses. The room was beginning to take on the coppery smell of blood and the odour of bodily fluids having been released in terror. It was all Joe could do not to gag.

"As for your friend, however… he's coming with me."

For the first time since being brought downstairs, Archard opened his eyes and looked at Maxine. "Why? What do you need me for?"

"Really?" came her incredulous response. "You're kidding, right? Didn't you hear a word I just said? My father was Obadiah Stark. You were one of the last people to see him alive… well, dead too. I want you to show me where you took him."

Archard shook his head vigorously. "I can't," he said insistently. "I really can't. They'd kill me… The Brethren would kill me."

Maxine walked towards him, the length of her dress making it look as though she were gliding across the floor. "That's terrible," she said in a trembling falsetto voice, wiping the blade of the still-bloodied knife on the shoulder of his jacket. "And what do you think I'm going to do to you if you don't?"

"Where's Lamont?" Joe interrupted, looking around the room.

He hadn't noticed him leave. "Where's Sim?"

"Oh, he had to see a man with your dog. That's what we tell people when we don't want them to know what we're doing, isn't it, Joe?"

"If you hurt her…" he began to say, recognising her jibe at his message for her in Sim's flat.

"YOU'LL WHAT?" Maxine's voice reverberated off the dank basement walls, the aggression behind it catching Joe off-guard.

Her face was twisted into something he could only describe as desolate and bereft of any compassion whatsoever - a distant cry from the woman he'd slept with.

A shudder ran up and down his spine as he remembered their night together. Her composure regained after taking a deep breath, Maxine spoke again in a voice that belied what had just occurred. "So, as I was saying, Gideon is going to come with me and you shall be left here to your own devices. *But beware, beware, The Broker's here, a name to give you shivers. And if he catches you tonight, he'll peel your skin in slivers.* Hmm, not bad. Made that up on the spot."

She laughed to herself and grabbed hold of Archard's arm, directing him to the corner of the basement.

Joe moved slightly, considering making a grab for her and the knife. As though sensing his intent, Maxine spoke without turning around. "Don't bother. If I'm not where I'm supposed to be later, your friend dies."

Joe stumbled back and slid down the wall slowly, fatigue overwhelming him.

"Oh and don't worry about the mess," Maxine instructed

as she opened a hidden door against the back of the room, pushing Archard through ahead of her. "You might want to leave soon though, the smell of dead people after a while, phew. Then again, he's roaming about somewhere… I'll let you decide what's best."

The brick-mottled door slid shut behind them and Joe was alone. He looked around the room, trying to comprehend what he'd just witnessed, entombed in a silence so pervasive he thought he might suffocate, surrounded by the signs of incalculable suffering and torture.

He used the wall as leverage to aid his rise to his feet and stepped closer to the bodies nearest to him, his legs wobbling beneath him. Joe knew there was nothing he could do to help them, but needed to check. Given what Maxine had told him before she'd left, he would rather stay here amongst the offal and desecrated souls than face whatever was waiting for him.

Joe realised what a fool he'd been, not just regarding the ease by which he'd allowed Maxine to seduce him but that he hadn't pieced it together sooner. Rebecca, Lamont's taunts regarding The Brethren, the inexplicable appearance of Maxine at his door that evening… it all added up to one huge 'you gotta be fuckin' kiddin' me!' and yet he'd been ignorant of all the evidence.

Maybe he'd subconsciously wanted to be.

The reporter in him wasn't gone but certainly neutered, mostly by choice; partly by circumstance. He'd wanted to leave it all behind, but his obsession with The Brethren had proven too much to ignore. And now there was this Broker in the mix. By default, if he was called The Broker then he dealt in something, trafficked something.

What was it Maxine had said? '*He procured all of these.*' He dealt in people as a commodity.

That was his business.

Sounds of floorboards creaking above him froze his blood. Was this it? Him?

Joe stood up as quickly as he was able and strode across the room, taking up a position around the corner. He glanced around and looked for the lever that Maxine had used to open the hidden door, feeling around the wall to see if he might dislodge something but found nothing.

Figures. My first secret passage and I can't get in the fucker.

He heard the door at the top of the stairs squeal on its hinges as it was opened, followed by footsteps heading downwards. His breathing was increasing so rapidly he wondered if he'd be able to stifle it enough to go unheard. Sweat accumulated across his neck and down his back, the trickling sensation making him itchy.

They were in the basement with him – two people. Judging by the sharp intake of breath and murmuring, he guessed they were both men.

Two men.

She only said *The* Broker.

Singular.

But he might have help, someone to assist in his work. Joe didn't dare make his presence known in case whoever was sharing the charnel room with him wasn't friendly.

The next words he heard helped him decide.

"You two better had come down here."

'To the last I grapple with thee; from hell's heart I stab at thee; for hate's sake I spit my last breath at thee.'

Herman Melville

||||| ||||| |||| ||||| ||||| ||| |||

HEATHER AND ALEX MADE THEIR WAY DOWN THE STAIRS, stifling gags and holding their noses as the smell of death drifted up from below.

"Jesus," was Heather's only response as she surveyed the horror around her. At least 20 bodies were positioned around the perimeter of the basement, all mutilated to varying degrees of severity, all having obviously suffered horrific deaths.

Halliday nodded to his partner to begin checking the victims and moved off to check the back of the room. He'd only taken a few steps forward when he saw a shape move out from around the corner. He raised his HK416 assault rifle and shouted out. "DON'T MOVE. Come out with your hands raised… NOW!"

Joe shuffled slowly into the light, his hands above his head. He saw Heather and Alex and shrugged his shoulders apologetically.

"Christ, O'Connell," Heather exclaimed. "You could have been killed!" She shook her head slowly.

"Stand down, Commander. He's with me."

Halliday eyed up Joe suspiciously but lowered his weapon and stepped cautiously to the side to allow him passage. Joe uttered a thank you as he walked towards Heather, relaxing his arms as he moved.

"You stupid bastard!" she admonished him before her face relaxed and took on a look of concern. "Are you okay? Are you hurt?"

"Okay, no," Joe replied with a heavy sigh. "Injured, no."

He moved and sat on the bottom step slowly as though every bone in his body ached. "You need to catch these fuckers, Heather. What they've done… well, you can see. They only left just before you arrived. You must have walked right by them.

"Detective," Halliday said, breaking the stillness. "You'd better secure this gentleman. We'll ensure it's safe for the SOCO's and forensics and feedback anything we find to you."

Heather continued to stare at Joe, visually processing a multitude of potential rejoinders. After what seemed like an age, she spoke. "Come on. Upstairs. We can debrief at the station."

Joe moved eagerly, keen to get away from the desecration around him. He moved behind Alex and ahead of Heather as they made their way up to the kitchen area, his legs feeling like lead weights. He stumbled at the top, Heather reaching forward to steady him.

"Thank you."

Expecting no response, he pulled out one of the chairs closest to him and sat down. He placed his forehead on the table, savouring its cool surface against his skin. The memories of the screaming and ungodly howling were still reverberating around his head, complimenting the visions of torment assaulting his mind.

Bile burned in the back of his throat as the shrieking excess of the Obadians' butchery flicked past his mind's eye like flash cards. Resisting the urge to vomit, Joe opened his eyes and turned to look at Heather.

"They took Simone and Archard, Maxine did. They left via a passage down there… no idea where it leads. You need to find them. She wants to know what they did with her father's body… The Brethren… where they took him after they'd killed him that night. However bad this is, I don't think this is the end."

Heather was moving the chair nearest to him when her neck exploded in a shower of blood, her carotid artery ruptured by the copper encased lead bullet fired from the back door. She fell to the floor, opening her mouth as if to scream but no sound escaped.

Joe sprang to his feet in confusion just as Alex raced to Heather's side. She was about to lift her head and apply pressure to the neck wound when she was hit twice in the face. Her jaw and cheeks exploded in fragments of bone and muscle as the bullets passed through from one side to the other. Alex's eyes held a surprised expression as though she couldn't comprehend having been shot.

There was shouting from the basement, indistinguishable due to its ferocity and overlapping, but Joe knew it was the two ERU members reacting to the gunshots they'd just heard. Racing up the stairs, Halliday appeared first, just shy of the doorway to ensure he wasn't easy to spot for the assailant. Atkins was visible just behind him in a crouched position a few stairs down.

Halliday motioned with a flat hand for Joe to drop to the floor as he was currently stood looking dumbstruck and the proverbial sitting duck.

Following the instruction, Joe got into a prone position alongside Alex's body. He couldn't help but stare at the gaping cavity that had once been the lower part of her face and found himself once again fighting back nausea.

Halliday gestured towards Atkins and slowly moved out of the doorway on his haunches, checking all the lines of sight he could. Knowing where the shots had come from given where the bodies had fallen, he moved low and carefully around the corner and towards the front of the house.

Joe intermittently glanced between him and Atkins, intent on following whatever instructions they gave him. Despite all his experience as a journalist, he'd never personally been in a situation involving firearms. The Troubles had become less intense and were just beginning to be fought on the political battlefield when he'd got his job at the paper, so it was just a circumstance he'd never experienced.

Halliday had been out of sight for a few minutes when they heard the crack of a gunshot from outside.

Atkins signalled for Joe to stay put and spoke over his headset. "Tango Leader, come in. Over."

Static.

"Tango Leader, come in. Over." Static.

"Anyone, respond. Over."

Atkins pushed at his combat helmet, trying to wipe the sweat from the top of his forehead. Securing it back into position, he moved up the few remaining stairs and out into the kitchen, taking up a low position beside Joe.

"Don't move," he instructed. "Understood?"

Joe just nodded. Atkins moved onto his stomach and leopard-crawled towards the open back door. He dragged some blood with him as he went, leaving a trail as though an exsanguinating slug.

Joe shimmied around slightly and saw Atkins taking up a position at the door. He turned and nodded at Joe, indicating he was about to venture out when a shadow fell over him. Looking up slowly, he saw a well-built man in a black jacket towering over him, a SIG Sauer P226 in his hand and an empty, vacant look in his eyes.

The muzzle flashed twice, the front of Atkins' head splitting open like a melon. Exposed brain matter was visible where his helmet had been. His body slumped like a rag doll's, his fingers still clutching his weapon. A pool of sticky warm blood began coalescing around his body, his legs twitching like someone coming to the end of a seizure.

Joe wasn't entirely certain how he felt. He thought he could have come up with at least a few adjectives to describe everything he'd witnessed in the last hour, but his mind was simply a lump of clay.

The smell of death hung in the air as Joe struggled to his feet, his whole body a visual example of defeat. He knew there was nowhere he could go. Running wasn't an option and he didn't think the other officers Heather and Alex must have come with were still alive.

He heard the assailant moving across the kitchen towards him, his footsteps heavy on the laminate floor. Joe closed his eyes and took a deep breath. When he opened them, the man was standing in directly in front of him.

"They with you?" he asked. "I hope not because they're all dead."

"Go fuck yourself."

Joe saw him reach into his pocket and then a flash in front his eyes before he felt a sharp prick on his neck. Almost instantly the room swayed and reconfigured itself as though becoming an interpretive example of the Penrose stairs.

He thought of Sim and how he'd let her down, imagining she'd only suffer for his curiosity. He even considered Archard and what his fate might entail at the hands of The Tally Man's daughter.

Joe felt himself falling and floating in the strangeness that was eternity and then there was only an enduring darkness.

'There is no hunting like the hunting of man, and those who have hunted armed men long enough and liked it, never care for anything else thereafter.'

Ernest Hemingway

NOW

||||| ||||||||| |||||||||||| |||||

"GO FUCK YOURSELF."

Those had been Joe O'Connell's last words before finding himself here.

Drifting back from unconsciousness, he returned from darkness only to find himself engulfed in a different kind— one that was virtually pitch black and imbued with a musty, dank smell.

He tried to lift himself from the seated position he was in, straining against the leather straps securing him in place. Iron ankle fetters tethered his legs tightly against what he recognised was a chair. His fingers felt around the arms to see if he could create any give in the straps but he gave up after a minute or so. Something cold and hard was pressing against the soles of his feet. It took him a few moments to realise his shoes and socks had been removed and that the stone floor was the source of the chill.

Adrenaline shot through his body, jolting him back into a hyper-aware state. His muscles, though appearing to be unresponsive, had retained their innate ability to twitch and contract, causing him to shiver in the chill of the cold air. His memory sluggish, he briefly recalled where he had been before here—the house—and visualised seeing Maxine in front of him. He remembered the pressure of the needle as it had punctured the skin of his neck and the soft call of insentience as it engulfed him.

Joe began to writhe about violently with no effect. The chair remained static as though fastened to the floor. His eyes were still adjusting to the gloom of his surroundings. He screwed them up a few times to see if it would help him focus and make sense of anything.

He was able to discern his location was either a storage container or perhaps a huge silo. There were slatted windows on either side of him but no light through them, meaning either they were covered or it was night-time.

It felt like night, though he couldn't articulate why. Perhaps his somnolent state was due to the residual effects of whatever he'd been sedated with to get him here. As if on cue, the injection site began to throb and he attempted to angle his neck in order to rub it against his shoulder. It wasn't as effective as scratching with a finger, but it would have to do. Joe knew he had much bigger problems to worry about.

Part of him wondered whether he was dreaming. That he was somehow in the middle of a nightmare he was yet to wake from. Recent events rolled around his mind - Etchison, the Branch Obadians… Maxine - but he failed to see how any of them could have led to this.

Being here. In this room.

As a child, he'd always been terrified of the dark.

Nyctophobia. The word itself had always reminded him of a creature lurking within the night's obsidian embrace. A nyctophobe… a nyctosaur. He'd come up with all sorts of names for them, supine creatures that lurked beneath your bed or in the wardrobe.

He could feel it rising now, the grinding anxiety that accompanied that fear, the most basic of limiting mechanisms to prevent reckless behaviour in the most extreme of circumstances. An evolutionary advantage which prevented you from running around the African desert like a lunatic when there were lions present.

His fear of the dark had never prompted an acute fight or flight response. Instead, it had always developed more like a foreboding prescience, creeping up from the base of his spine and slowly enveloping his chest like an anaconda squeezing the very breath from his body. Ironically, that increasing anxiety also augmented situational awareness, making someone finely attuned to danger and able to respond to environmental cues when their wellbeing might be in danger.

No shit.

Fear—a gnawing emotion, honed over millennia by both nature and nurture so that it had become a systematic and instinctive survival response that could prepare you for the world and ensure that you'd intuitively do whatever you needed to do to survive - to live another day.

Or die another day.

Either way, fear was the body's way of making certain you never forgot what was needed to go on living. Oddly, none of that was helpful as Joe sat here with a hunch that what was about to follow would be painful… and possibly fatal.

An old Simon and Garfunkel lyric inexplicably popped into his head relating to the welcoming of darkness.

He heard breathing in the obscurity before a light blinked on above him, causing phosphenes to appear in bursts before his eyes. His vision blurred, and he could just make out someone standing in front of a table at the end of the room. He could also make out the figure patiently laying out a variety of medical implements that Joe knew weren't there to help him with his ingrowing toenail. Joe recognised him as the man from the house… the one in the kitchen who'd taken out an entire armed response team and two officers. Only now Joe could see he was built like a rugby player, the muscles on his arms threatening to rip through his tightly buttoned black jacket.

"So, that's how far we've come," announced the man gently in a soft British accent, his back still to Joe. "Heroism has gone from a rallying cry or profound statement to '*go fuck yourself* '? And you call yourself a journalist. Shame on you."

"Get bent," Joe snorted derisively, straining futilely once again at his restraints.

"You've the potential to cause me a great deal of trouble, Joseph. I wanted to kill you back at the house. Maybe I did and you're in Hell."

His right hand floated over the various items as though trying to decide which one to choose. He settled on a scalpel and turned back to face Joe, his face hidden in the shadows.

"I'll never tell you whatever it is you want to know," Joe stated emphatically. "Besides, I met Obadiah Stark. I can already tell you're a rank amateur compared to him. I don't even think you'd be interesting enough to make him sick."

The man stepped forward and pressed the scalpel against the right-hand side of Joe's neck in one, swift motion. His black hair was cut close to his head, flashes of grey along the temple. Freckles peppered his tanned face, vivid blue eyes belaying clarity of purpose. His mouth was turned up slightly as though trying to force a smile.

"This area I'm pressing against is called Erb's point, named after Wilhelm Heinrich Erb who located it. It's basically where the four nerves of the cervical plexus meet. And if I just make a small incision here…"

Joe cried out as the scalpel slid into his neck, severing the nerve cluster with the immediate effect of making his right arm tingle as though it had been immersed in freezing cold water. He felt it go limp, his hand automatically rotating and flexing up and over as though gesturing for a tip.

"…you'll find you're paralysed down your right arm. Incidentally, this injury affects the circulation, which means your arm will no longer be able to regulate its temperature, so in cold weather, it'll hurt like a son of a bitch."

Joe grimaced against the pain migrating from his neck and up and down his right side. His body shook with adrenaline, though he imagined his old friend fear was also playing a part.

"You know," the stranger said, his voice lilting softly. "I've never actually killed anyone before, not like this. Yes, guns and bullets, but not one-on-one so to speak. I've never even put a finger on those cattle I procure for my clients. You would be my first… breaking me in so to speak. Your actions have potentially damaged my reputation. It's that reputation which has contributed to the confidence of my clientele in dealing with me, knowing I'll provide them with a superior product, exactly as requested. And, in one deft move, you could have FUCKED IT ALL UP!"

The man began shaking, hitting himself on the head in frustration. Joe couldn't help but smile at the fact that his actions, despite the pain and fear he was feeling, were having such a profound effect. He just wished he knew who his assailant was.

"So what happens now?" Joe asked glibly. "I say sorry, you let me go with my limp arm and we call it quits?"

"I admire your ability to find humour, even in such a desperate state," the stranger announced, the angry tremble in his voice rapidly receding. "It's endearing actually. But you know what's about to happen. You'll be tortured and tell me what I've been paid to find out."

"Which is what exactly?" Joe countered.

"The truth. And I have something that'll help you locate it."

"I'll die before I tell you anything," Joe stated defiantly.

"Oh, I know you will," his aggressor announced proudly. "Die that is."

He moved back to the table and swapped the scalpel for a series of bamboo slivers before moving to the back of the room out of Joe's sight.

The sound of a chair being dragged echoed around the room before the man appeared before him and sat down, rocking the chair forward slightly so that they were directly in front of each other. He ran a finger along the tops of the bamboo, the motion making a barely audible clicking sound that Joe found extremely disturbing.

He felt sweat beginning to build up on the back of his neck, his increasing respirations causing him to feel lightheaded. Joe realised his irrational fear of the dark had been just a minor apprehension compared to this. If he didn't know better, he would have said he was having a panic attack. Joe suddenly found himself wondering if it was possible to die from fear.

The man selected one of the bamboo slivers, placing the others on the table to his left. He positioned it just below the index finger nail of Joe's right hand.

"In case you haven't guessed yet, this is going to hurt… a lot."

Maxine watched with fascination at the scene unfolding before her.

A myriad of equipment was connected to Joe O'Connell on the other side of the viewing screen; infusion devices and monitoring equipment, some of which Maxine suspected were prototypes, were carefully positioned around Joe with a specific function to perform.

Gideon Archard moved beside Maxine, his face fraught with anxiety. "They'll kill us both if they know we're here, you realise that, don't you?"

Maxine smirked nonchalantly. "They can try."

She took a step closer to the viewing window before

speaking again. "So, this is where you brought my father? This is what you did to him?"

Archard cleared his throat. "Well, it was more complicated than that, but essentially, yes."

"Was he in pain?" Her voice was low and solemn.

"Not in the physical sense. The relatives of his victims felt his prison sentence and sanctioned execution didn't constitute justice, so they came to us and asked for him to… erm…"

"Suffer," Maxine said for him.

"Yes, indeed." Archard was shuffling nervously. "This facility contains equipment that can induce a dream state where the individual can be made to experience whatever is felt appropriate. In your father's case, it was remorse. The relatives felt he could only understand their loss if he learnt to love and then lose something himself."

"This equipment can do all of that?"

"And more besides, but that's its main function. It takes an individual's own fears, dreams, longings etc. and uses them to form an elaborate dreamscape in which they experience whatever it is their mind is forcing them to. At least, that's how I understand it."

"So, O'Connell could be experiencing…"

"Something wonderful, something horrifying… hard to know. From the expression on his face, I'd hazard a guess it's something very far from pleasant… very far indeed."

Maxine placed a hand on the glass and stared longingly at Joe. "I won't let you suffer long, my dear. Just enough for you to understand."

She quickly composed herself and turned to Archard. "So, my father. Take me to him."

Archard hesitated."What do you intend to do? I told you it isn't just Stark down there. We have a number of people in cryogenic stasis, not all of whom are dead. If I'm going to die because of this, I'd like to know what your plan is for them."

"You'll see," she replied, her eyes glinting with dark promise. "Very well," Archard said, indicating the direction they'd be heading in.

As they made their way down a clinically white corridor, Maxine felt a thrill of excitement rising from her gut. She was about to meet the man hidden from her for so much of her life. She'd understood her mother's reasoning for keeping his identity a secret. Her life would have been hell if anyone had known she'd given birth to the child of a serial killer.

But that was all prologue. Today defined a new dawn for the Obadians and all they stood for – all *he* had stood for.

Archard stopped in front of a large, steel door, his hand hovering over the electronic keypad. "You realise this is Pandora's Box. Once we open it, they'll be no sealing it again."

Maxine nodded enthusiastically. "Oh, I understand. Please proceed."

Archard shrugged and reluctantly entered the six-digit code. A hiss of escaping gas broke the seal, chilling the air around them. Archard pulled the door open to reveal a metal stairway leading down.

He was about to take a step forward when he felt Maxine's

hand on his arm. Turning to face her, he noticed a look in her eyes that made him suddenly feel sick. He knew that the response he gave to the question she was about to ask would decide his fate in the next few seconds.

"My father," she asked. "Is he alive?"

Archard considered his answer carefully.

"Well, let's find out together."

AFTERWORD

NAMELESS is the product of a lot of sleepless nights, hours of research into cults and a desperation to write something that was completely different to *Hellbound* yet set in the same universe (think Marvel movies; different characters mostly, but interconnected!).

Is it any good? I shall let you, dear readers, decide the answer to an author's favourite question. As for the characters, many of them are named after competition winners, willing participants, friends and one leader of a small, innocuous, sparsely membered group called The Book Club. The remainder are either returning characters or figments of my imagination.

As is sometimes the way with writing, though the places in Nameless are real, for the sake of narrative I have condensed some of the details. No offence is meant nor intended.

Some of the other elements within Nameless however, specifically that of cults, are based on organisations and religions that are real (minus the murder and sacrifice, of course). Most are harmless and perhaps even beneficial to those who struggle to find their place in life. Others are not so altruistic. If you know of anyone who has been the victim of a cult or are a relative of someone previously or currently a cult member, know that there are many organisations and charities to help and offer support to those who have been affected by the harmful methods of cults.

The most notable is the Cult Information Centre in London who can be contacted on 0845 4500 868

Any mistakes in Nameless are my own.

ABOUT THE AUTHOR

David trying hard to look intelligent and
natural... and failing only to look smug

David McCaffrey was born in Middlesbrough, raised in
West Sussex and now lives in Redcar. He worked in the
NHS for many years, his last position being Lead Nurse in
Infection Prevention and Control at James Cook
University
Hospital.
He started writing following the birth of his first son and in
2010 was accepted onto the writing coach programme run
by Steve Alten, international bestselling author of *Meg* and
The Mayan Prophecy. *Hellbound* was the result and the rest, as
they say, is history (cliche, cliche).
Though psychological thrillers are his *raison d'etre*, David is
also an activist for bullying and harassment in the NHS.

His book, 'Do No Harm: Bullying and Harassment in the NHS' went to Number One in the Nursing and White Collar Crime categories of Amazon Kindle charts in November 2018 and was the Number One bestselling book in the U.S Amazon Kindle charts for more than three weeks in the Issues, Trends and Roles category.

David is a proud supporter and donator to the Ben Cohen StandUp Foundation which tackles bullying across the board, from schools to the workplace. He had the honour of being invited to speak at the Standup Foundation's Inaugural Conference in November 2018.

Half of all profits from 'Do No Harm' go to the Ben Cohen Foundation.

David lives with his wife Kelly, has a Jakey, a Liam (a.k.a Gruffy) and a Cole (a.k.a Baby Moo Man) They also have an Obi… who's the dog.

42006191R00193

Printed in Poland
by Amazon Fulfillment
Poland Sp. z o.o., Wrocław